Faith

Along the

Volga

Merribeth Bruntz

ISBN 979-8-89309-545-6 (Paperback)
ISBN 979-8-89309-546-3 (Digital)

Covenant Books
11661 Hwy 707
Murrells Inlet, SC 29576
www.covenantbooks.com

CHAPTER

1

Hamburg, 1764

Maria heard footsteps on her front porch. *Who could be here?* she wondered. She wasn't expecting anyone, and she never had guests. No one did, as there were barely any people left in town.

Suddenly, the front door opened. The man in the doorway looked familiar. He had a beard and was quite thin. He was staring at her. Could this be her Christoph? He had been gone over two years, and she had heard nothing from him since he left.

"Christoph?" she asked.

"Yes," he replied.

She ran into his arms and his tender embrace.

"I've missed you so much, my darling," she cried. "I thought I would never see you again."

"Believe me, I feared the same," he replied.

"I prayed night and day for your safe return."

"God brought me home to you, my love."

It had been over two years since Christoph was conscripted to serve in the German army at the age of thirty-eight to fight in the seven-year war. He and Maria had no children, so it was just a matter of time before he would be called upon to fight. It appeared Germany had been at war with someone for centuries.

His brother, Wilhelm, had died in the 1740s while serving in the military. Wilhelm was ten years older than Christoph, and Maria was married to Wilhelm when he died. The family loved Maria, and even though she was ten years older than Christoph, he found her quite attractive with her beautiful blond hair and blue eyes. Maria and Wilhelm had no children, which made the situation easier. After a brief courtship, Christoph and Maria married in 1744.

Christoph was a second-generation gardener. His grandfather had left rural farming near the end of the thirty-year war. Their land was seized when they were unable to pay the ever-increasing taxes that were levied to fund the war. Also, there had been many years of poor crop production because of shortened growing seasons. The weather had been too cool and damp to have a high yield. So the family moved near Hamburg to the village of Liograd.

It was easy for Christoph's grandfather to transition from farming to gardening, and there was a need for talented gardeners to work on the palace grounds. The gardens in Hamburg were modelled after the fabled palace gardens of King Louis XIV at Versailles, and it required a special creative talent to create and maintain such beauty.

Christoph's father, Georg, was trained to follow in the footsteps of his father. And Christoph was trained by Georg. Wilhelm was always more interested in military service. The same could not be said for Christoph. When he received his notice of forced conscription, he thought his life had ended. Worse yet, he wondered what would happen to Maria if he died.

But he returned, and he was ready to return to the life he and Maria had before his dreadful experience in the war. Maybe they could finally have a baby. Maybe life would get easier for them now that Germany was at peace.

Christoph came home to one piece of bad news. His mother, Catharine, fell ill with typhus while he was gone. She was living with Maria, but there was nothing she could do to save her. His father, Georg, had died of a stroke in 1750, so Christoph had been managing the gardens by himself for over ten years when the military came calling.

"I have to go see Johann in the morning and start working in the gardens again," Christoph said.

"What will you do if they have no work?" asked Maria. "After all, there has been no one to do the work since you and the other men went off to war."

"We will cross that bridge when we get to it," he replied.

* * * * *

The next morning, Christoph went to see Johann, and the news was bad but not totally bad. Christoph could return to gardening at the palace, but his pay would be reduced drastically. There was nothing he could do but work and hope his pay would increase.

Of course, Maria was not happy when she heard this. She had been selling extra food that she grew in their vegetable garden at the local market. That money, plus the small wages that Christoph made while at war, helped her survive, but now they would need all their food and there would be no money from the military. She would have to be smart about putting up food for the winter, or they would starve.

The next morning, Christoph joined Johann in the palace gardens. It was a warm June day, and there was much work to be done. Johann pruned bushes, while Christoph deadheaded the palace rose gardens. The work continued throughout the week. At the end of the week, Christoph received his wages. They were half of what he earned before his military conscription. When he got home, Maria was very worried. She feared they would not survive the winter.

"We need to plow more ground so we can grow more crops," she said.

"I will start first thing in the morning," he replied.

The next morning, Christoph began plowing the remaining portions of their unused ground behind the house. He then planted the remaining vegetable seeds. They would have a good crop if the weather cooperated. Too much rain might cause the root crops to rot in the ground.

Throughout the summer, Christoph continued to work with Johann, and Maria managed the home garden and took care of two pigs and three chickens. One of the pigs would likely be butchered and the meat smoked for storage during the winter. If any of the chickens stopped producing eggs, they would suffer the same fate. By the end of the summer, she was pickling and drying vegetables and making apple cider from the apples off their apple tree. By fall, she had pickled carrots, peas, beans, cucumbers, and beets. She also stored turnips, potatoes, and onions in the root cellar with eggs from the chickens.

One evening she told Christoph, "I think we will survive the winter, God willing."

"That's wonderful. You have worked so hard this fall," he replied. "I have faith that God will take care of us."

Christoph thought Maria was truly remarkable. She worked constantly, which was no small feat for a woman that was fifty years old. While he was at war, she took care of his aging mother and maintained their home and small plot of land all by herself. Johann had periodically checked in with her, and he was extremely impressed at how well she managed everything.

The winter of 1764 was bitter cold with more snow and ice than usual. They had to butcher their last pig and two of their three chickens to survive. Since Christoph wasn't working in the gardens all winter, there was no money coming in, and they ran out of what they had saved. They knew that they couldn't continue to live this way.

On Sundays, they attended church when the weather allowed. Everyone was struggling. As they left church one Sunday, Christoph expressed his frustration with the sermon. "Every week we hear about the struggles of the Israelites in the wilderness and how they had to maintain their faith in God," he told Maria. "Things are so bad here that I fear that I'm losing my faith."

"Christoph, you must keep your faith in God. He will take care of us," replied Maria.

He nodded his head, but he didn't know if he agreed with her.

CHAPTER

2

April 1765

There was a foreigner in the market in the center of the village. Christoph saw the crowd gathering as he was walking to work in the gardens.

The foreigner was Russian, and he was handing out leaflets written in German. He was shouting about the manifesto of Empress Catherine II of Russia. There was to be a meeting, and the date, time, and place was announced in the leaflet. Christoph took one of the leaflets and headed to work.

When Christoph arrived home that evening, he showed the leaflet to Maria.

"I think I should go to this meeting and see what this is all about," he said.

"What could the Empress of Russia want with Germans? It might be a total waste of time," she replied.

"Well, we will know when I go to the meeting. It's this Saturday afternoon, and I'm going to go to it."

When Christoph arrived at the meeting on Saturday after spending the morning in the gardens, the foreigner started by reading the decree of Empress Catherine II.

"By the Grace of God, we, Catherine II, empress and autocratic leader of all of Holy Russia..." It explained in detail the conditions for a foreign immigration proposed for Christian Germans to colonize the large uninhabited areas of the vast Russian Empire. The foreigner, whose name was Dmitri Ivanov, told those gathering that there would be money for transportation. When they arrived in Russia, there would be money to buy land, animals, seed, and tools.

This would be payable after ten years, without interest. There would be tax exemption for thirty years. There would be religious freedom and no forced conscription into military service.

Dmitri continued to describe the journey to Russia. He told them that they would leave in groups of no more than thirty, go by wagon from Hamburg to Lübeck, and from there take a ship to Russia, which would take about ten days. They would pay nothing for the whole trip. Also, once they reached St. Petersburg, they would either depart by boat via the Volga River to Saratov, or by land, going through Novgorod; Tver, Moscow; and other cities. Upon arrival, they would be sent to where they chose to live, either in the city or to their farm to plow the land.

At the end of the meeting, Dmitri Ivanov wanted to interview all who wished to go. This meant that Christoph needed to make a quick decision. He wouldn't be able to talk to Maria about this before he made the decision. He listened to the conversations around him. He was reminded of the harsh winter he and Maria had just endured, and he had no idea if he could make enough money in the gardens this summer. Maria would be fifty-one this year, and he would be forty-one. Who knew if they would ever have another opportunity like this.

So Christoph decided to make the decision to leave. He stood in line to be interviewed by Dmitri Ivanov. When it was his turn, Dmitri asked him some questions.

"What is your last name?" he asked.

"My last name is Bauer," Christoph replied.

"Are you a farmer, or do you have a trade?"

"I'm a gardener, but I come from a farming background."

"You will be a farmer. We have no use for a gardener. We need farmers," said Dmitri. Christoph nodded in agreement.

"Do you have a family?"

"Yes, my wife, Maria. We have no children."

"The trip will be strenuous, so it is best that you have no children," replied Dmitri.

When Dmitri had finished interviewing all who wished to go to Russia, he gave them instructions. "In one month, we will leave at first light. We will travel via wagon to Lübeck. Bring clothes for the cold, food, and all your money. And bring nothing heavy."

Christoph left the meeting wondering how he was going to tell Maria what he had just done. She was very strong-willed, and he sensed that this may not go over well. He was going to have to stand his ground with her because he knew they couldn't go through another winter like the last one.

When he got home, he told Maria about the meeting and that he had decided to sign them up for departure. Maria took the news rather calmly. She liked the idea of going to a place where they could start over and not have to deal with the threat of war or religious persecution. Christoph assured her that he could handle farming, and she really liked the idea of no forced conscription into the military. The only thing that concerned her was the journey. It sounded like they would be traveling forever.

"I'm sure we will be there before winter," Christoph told her.

They agreed that they would leave, and they began their preparations the next morning.

"So what is going to become of our home?" asked Maria the next morning.

"I've been thinking of asking Ludwig Hess if he would like to purchase the property from us," replied Christoph. "His son is getting married this summer, and I've heard that they will be living with Ludwig and his wife unless they find property."

"You've really thought this through, haven't you? How long have you wanted to leave here?"

"When I was fighting in the war, I decided I wanted to leave this country. I was tired of all the wars and all the fighting over religion, but I had no idea where we could go until now," responded Christoph. "Besides, maybe this is God taking care of us. We have been praying for ways to survive. Maybe this is God's answer."

The following week, Christoph spoke with Ludwig. It didn't take long for them to negotiate a price because Ludwig was eager to have property for his son, and Christoph was eager to sell out and leave.

Maria and Christoph spent the next three weeks preparing to leave. They were able to pack the belongings that they would take into two small bags. They took warm clothes, some food, and the money that Christoph received from the sale of the property.

CHAPTER

3

On an early Saturday morning in May, they started their journey. They met the other travelers in the market square in the center of their village. They were loaded onto the wagons with their baggage. There were thirty-five men, women, and children that left Hamburg for the journey to Lübeck. The trip took three days. They stayed in villages along the way. At one point, the wagons became stuck in muddy ruts, so they had to unload the wagons and carry their baggage.

"I'm sure glad that we only have two small bags," stated Maria.

"Yes, this is why we traveled so light," replied Christoph. Christoph worked with the other men to push the wagons out of the mud, while Maria carried their baggage. Fortunately, about a mile down the road, the dirt was dry again.

On the day they arrived in Lübeck, they found large crowds waiting to board the ships to Russia. They spent the next three weeks waiting to continue their travels. They were forced to live in overcrowded barracks, which were filthy and rodent-infested. Plus, there were plenty of people who would take advantage of anyone they could. They received money from the Russian agents responsible for transporting them to Russia while they waited, which was a good thing, as they had run out of the food they brought from Hamburg.

"You must stay with me at all times, as we can trust no one," Christoph told Maria.

Maria was horrified by the behavior of some of these people. She had seen several who had been beaten by others to steal their money.

"I hope we don't have to live with these kinds of people when we get to Russia," she told Christoph.

Finally, the day arrived for their departure to Russia. Christoph and Maria boarded a small packet ship with approximately forty others to sail across the Baltic Sea to Kronstadt, Russia. The voyage was 450 miles and took fifteen days. Christoph and Maria had never traveled on a ship over open water. Both struggled the first couple of days trying to move about the ship while it navigated the rough sea. About the time Christoph adjusted to the rocking about, Maria became very ill. She was vomiting up any food she ate.

"I don't know how I will finish the trip. I feel so weak," she told Christoph.

"You will make it, my love. I will not leave you. Let's pray."

The Lord is my shepherd. I shall not want. He maketh me to lie down in green pastures: he leadeth me beside still waters. He restoreth my soul: he leadeth me in the paths of righteousness for his name's sake. Yea, though I walk through the valley of the shadow of death, I will fear no evil: for thou art with me; thy rod and thy staff they comfort me. Thou preparest a table before me in the presence of mine enemies: thou anointest my head with oil; my cup runneth over. Surely goodness and mercy shall follow me all the days of my life: and I will dwell in the house of the Lord forever. (Psalm 23 KJV)

"Amen."

By the time they finished, several on the boat were praying.

Christoph stayed with Maria and received help from others when he went to get food for them. He watched other less fortunate people on the ship die. He thought that there must be something in the food or water that was making so many people sick. As they started to run out of money to purchase food, Maria and several others started to recover. Christoph thought to himself that the meat must be rancid. It probably wasn't salted enough for storage. He kept his thoughts to himself because this ship was the last place that he and Maria needed to be if a fight broke out. They used their remaining funds to purchase only vegetables and ate sparingly for the remaining days on the ship.

By the time they reached the port of Kronstadt, Maria felt much better. She was still weak, but she felt she could continue their journey. They were moved to a village called Oranienbaum, where they were given temporary housing. Over the next several days, they were required to complete paperwork by Russian emigration. They were then told that they would have to swear the oath of loyalty to the Russian crown as set down in the 1763 manifesto. They were told by the Russians that this would happen the next day and that they had traveled too far to back out. No one would take them back to Hamburg.

"Christoph, what have we done?" cried Maria. "We are going to become Russian subjects, and we can never return home."

Christoph was worried, but he didn't want Maria to see this.

"We agreed that we needed to move on to a new life because we had no future in Hamburg. This is part of our new life, and we will survive."

"You decided we needed a new life. I was willing to continue our life in Hamburg," she fired back.

"We are going to have to make this work because we can't go back," he replied.

There was silence between them that night; but the next morning was a new day, and they agreed to swear the oath of loyalty to the Russian Crown.

Before they took the oath, they were told the total amount of debt they owed to the Russian government for their travels thus far. The amount was shocking, and they were still very far from their destination. The debt continued to grow with each passing day, with the granting of financial advances during the transportation. Apparently, Dmitri Ivanov meant that they would pay nothing for the trip, for now. They were forced to sign a contract that regulated all goods and services due from Russia and the resultant rights and duties of each signing colonist. In ten years, they would pay for all of this.

They were told that, upon arriving at the settlements along the Volga River, they would receive more money for purchases, such as animals, home, barn, seed, and implements. All this money was to be repaid after ten years in three installments over three years. Fortunately, no interest was payable.

On the bright side, they would have the freedom to practice their Lutheran religion, and they would have relief from monetary taxation for the next thirty years. There would be no conscription into military service. Inheritance law was also defined. They were told that they were expected to behave as loyal subjects of Catherine II of Russia and that they would adhere to Russian laws and customs. Christoph and Maria looked at each other but said nothing. All of this was quite disturbing, but what could they do? So they swore the oath of loyalty and signed the contract.

Everyone was then packed onto small ships and transported to St. Petersburg. Once they arrived, they were told that they were to stay on the docked ship and that they would depart for their settlement in a couple of days. The delays worried Christoph because he anticipated needing to be at the settlement before winter. It was already August.

As the days on the docked ship dragged on, the anxiety amongst the passengers increased. Several fights broke out. Christoph tried to shelter Maria from the violence.

"I don't know how we are going to live with these kinds of people," she would say.

Then one morning, two Russian men boarded the ship. The passengers thought they were leaving, but that was not the case. They visited with all the passengers and gave them information about their settlement areas. When Christoph and Maria met with the Russian, they were told that they would settle in a village called Merkel. Everyone in the Merkel village was of the Lutheran religion, and they were all farmers. Merkel was located on the hillside of the Volga River. This was the west side of the river. Apparently, this side of the river was unpopulated, and they would farm the land with other settlers.

"I wish they would tell us when we are leaving," whispered Maria.

"I agree. At this rate we will never make it there by winter," responded Christoph.

They continued to wait on the ship for several more days. Then finally, in September 1765, their journey to their new settlement began. They left St. Petersburg by ship and sailed up the Neva River through the Shlisselburg Canal to Lake Ladoga. They had some cold, rainy days on the ship. Some of the settlers feared that soon, snow would be falling.

By the time they reached Lake Ladoga, it was snowing. Maria was terrified, as the ship was rocking in the wind. It was impossible to walk because the decks were so wet. By the time they reached the Volkhov River, the snow and wind had stopped, but it was very cold. The settlers were soaked in wet clothes and freezing. They had been packed on the ship for months, and now many were becoming sick. Maria started coughing more frequently, and finally, she couldn't speak without coughing. Christoph was worried that she may not make it to Novgorod, let alone to their new settlement.

Finally, the ship's captain announced that they would spend the rest of the winter in Novgorod. There would be medical care for the sick and housing for those who were not sick.

"When we reach Novgorod, they will take care of you," Christoph told Maria. She looked at him but said nothing. He touched her face; she was burning up. He started to get scared. Help couldn't come soon enough.

Maria was raced off the ship on a stretcher and carried to the medical barracks. Christoph ran behind them, but he was told to wait inside the doorway of the barracks. The Russian nurses removed Maria's wet clothes and placed her in a night shirt. She was wrapped in warm blankets, and cool, wet rags were placed on her forehead and face. She was coughing, but she coughed up nothing. Finally, she rested. The doctor talked to Christoph, but his German was limited. What he did understand was that Maria was very sick, and the doctor was uncertain whether she would live.

As Christoph walked to the temporary housing that was being provided, he wondered what he was thinking, dragging Maria halfway across the world. It was selfish of him to think that they should leave their homeland just because he was so disgusted with life. The trip was a lot longer than he thought, and heaven only knew what these settlements would look like. And now, the worst thing that could happen was happening. Maria was deathly ill. What would he do if she died?

For several days, Christoph was not allowed to see Maria. He tried not to panic, but sometimes he wanted to race into the medical barracks to see her.

He couldn't do anything else, so he prayed.

"Our father which art in heaven, hallowed be thy name. Thy kingdom come. Thy will be done on earth, as it is in heaven. Give us this day our daily bread. And forgive us our debts, as we forgive our debtors. And lead us not into temptation but deliver us from evil: For thine is the kingdom, and the power, and the glory forever. Amen."

He prayed the Lord's Prayer every day. Maria was the one who led them in prayer. He wasn't used to praying alone. Finally, after a week, he was allowed to see her. He was told that her fever had broken and that he could now talk to her.

"How are you, my darling?" he asked.

"I have pain in my chest, but that's probably because of all the coughing. I'm weak and can hardly catch my breath," she replied.

"You need to rest, dear. I've been told that we will be here until spring. It's been snowing since we arrived. You must get well. I've been praying every day. I don't know how I would survive without you. You have no idea how much I love you," said Christoph.

Maria smiled at him, and this gave him hope. The nurse indicated that it was time for him to leave so Maria could rest. Christoph kissed her on her forehead and left.

For the next two months, Maria remained in the medical barracks. Christoph visited every day. He was thankful that she was getting such good care. Slowly, her cough and chest pain subsided. By spring, her breathlessness had reduced, but she was still fatigued. She needed to work on her strength to continue the journey.

CHAPTER

4

Novgorod, April 1766

The snow had stopped, and the days were warmer when they boarded another ship to continue their journey. Maria was still a little weak, but she felt that she could continue, providing she didn't have to do much walking. Christoph had been assured by the Russian guides that she would ride in a wagon once they reached land.

They traveled up the Msta River to Vyshny Volochyok. From there, they would follow the land trail to the most northern navigable point of the Volga River at Torzhok. They arrived at Vyshny Volochyok in the afternoon, which allowed plenty of time for Christoph and the other men to load the wagons with their belongings. Christoph arranged a comfortable spot for Maria to ride in the wagon. The other women and children would ride in other wagons.

By this time, everyone knew how sick Maria had been, so they were very kind and helpful. It appeared that this group of settlers, all headed to Merkel village, were good people. Maria's earlier fears had all but subsided.

The next morning, the settlers left Vyshny Volochyok and began their travels to Torzhok. Christoph walked alongside the wagons with the other men. The sun was bright and the air warm. Conversation had been limited on the ships, but this was not the case this morning. The settlers were all Lutheran, and at one point they sang hymns, everyone enjoying being together. The land trail was muddy in spots, and occasionally, the women and children had to be unloaded from the wagons so the men could push them through the mud.

They traveled on the land trail for over two weeks, staying in villages along the way. Their Russian hosts were paid by their government to house the settlers in the villages along the way. Christoph and Maria were very grateful, but they were astonished to find that they were staying inside with chickens, sheep, pigs, and cattle.

"They must be having us stay in the barn with the animals," exclaimed Maria.

"No, this is not a barn. It's their house. We are all staying together with the animals," replied Christoph.

Even though Maria was riding in a wagon, she became more and more fatigued as the days wore on. She didn't know if she could make it to the settlement, but she hid this from Christoph as best she could.

Finally, they reached Torzhok. Christoph spent a couple of days helping the Russians and other male settlers load the ship in preparation for their trip to Saratov. Maria rested in the barracks provided for the settlers. There were other settlers who were also exhausted. Most of them were women, but there were also men who were not faring well. Maria had been very lucky to have survived the winter in Novgorod. There were several settlers who had died, and they had the same symptoms as Maria.

In the morning, they boarded the ship. The sun was bright, and the air was warm. The Volga River was amazingly smooth given its size. In some places, they couldn't see across it; it was so wide. The men on the ship were talking about the settlement they were traveling to, wondering if the land that they would be farming was along this magnificent river. There were many trees along the shore.

"Surely the land will be rich for planting," Christoph told Maria.

Maria agreed that it was a beautiful place, but she had her doubts about the land they were to receive from the Russians.

They were on the Volga River for almost two weeks. In the morning, they reached Saratov; they were sent to the government office where Christoph was issued seventy-five rubles, plus farm tools, and one cow and two pigs. Christoph loaded the farm tools into the wagon with Maria and the baggage. With the animals in tow, they made the final journey to the village of Merkel.

As it turned out, Merkel wasn't a village. The site of their destination left Christoph and Maria in shock. They were literally in a wilderness of tall grass with nothing else visible all around, except small trees. They couldn't believe that this was the grand paradise promised by Dmitri Ivanov back in Hamburg. The disappointment of finding a steppe that fulfilled none of their needs was unbearable.

Maria began to cry. "What have we done, Christoph? How will we survive? We have no home."

Christoph couldn't even answer. He just stared in disbelief. There were spaces for houses laid out, but there was nothing that could be used to build a house. They were told by the Russian guides that the wood to build the houses wasn't currently available locally, and they would have wood as soon as it was transported down the river to Saratov. Then it would have to be moved by horse and wagon to the various village sites.

The native Russian people living on the hillsides began to gather near the settlers. They couldn't understand what they were talking about, but they knew they were very upset. The Russians also could tell that these strange new people had no homes, for now. They tried to communicate with the settlers, and Christoph started to understand some of what was being said. The Russians were offering to house them until they could build homes of their own.

"Maria, they are offering to house us," said Christoph.

"Well, we can't sleep outside," she replied.

There was a tall Russian named Igor who lived up the hill from the settlement area marked for Christoph and Maria. He offered to house them. Igor went and got his horse and wagon and loaded Maria, the baggage, and the farm tools into the wagon. Igor led the horse and wagon up the hill, and Christoph followed him with the animals.

When they arrived, they saw a large hut built partially underground. There were several people living in the hut, as well as several farm animals. They had plenty of room for Christoph and Maria, plus their animals. Igor told Christoph that the hut was a *zemly-anka* and that they were taught how to build them by the wild tribes nearby. Igor offered to help Christoph build a hut for him and Maria tomorrow. Christoph appreciated the graciousness of the Russians, and he hoped Maria would too. He decided not to tell Maria about the wild tribes nearby. She was already upset enough.

* * * * *

The next morning, Igor and Christoph went back down the hill to the settlement area assigned to Christoph and Maria. They brought tools and a horse and wagon with them. It was August, so the days were warm and dry. They started digging a hole six feet deep. They put the dirt in the wagon and hauled it across the settlement site. It took several days, but they eventually had a hole big enough to contain a bedroom, kitchen, and sitting area around a woodstove.

The promised wood began to arrive at the settlement, so Christoph and Igor constructed an A-frame roof whose sides started on the ground at the rim of the hole. A pipe attached to the woodstove extended through the roof. They then put some of the dirt that they had dug up back on the roof. The back of the hut was built into the ground, and they used logs to create the front with a door that they could go down steps to open. They built a smaller hut to act as a barn for the animals that had a flat roof and no steps to the entrance.

While Christoph and Igor were building, Maria was working with the other women in the gardens, preparing food for winter storage. Igor's wife, Natalya, had a root cellar that was dug into one of the back corners of their hut so she would not have to leave the hut in the winter. Maria had become fast friends with Natalya.

Finally, by late October, Christoph and Maria were settled. Christoph and Igor were still helping other settlers when the first snow started. Many of them had to spend the first winter with the native Russians.

"This weather is something," said Christoph one sunny morning. "I expected snow all winter, like last winter. It snowed and was very cold for months."

"Yes, I know. One day it's snowing and the wind is blowing. And the next day, it's sunny and the snow is melting."

"It will be nice if it stays like this. It will be a lot easier to take care of the animals," replied Christoph.

By Christmas, it had gotten colder. In fact, it got frigid the week before. The snow stayed on the ground and wasn't melting. Christoph was still able to feed and water the animals daily. Maria didn't go out of the house.

In the settlement area next to Christoph and Maria lived Karl and Lena and their two children, Hans and Anna. Hans was fifteen and a great help to the men when they were building their *zemlyanka*. Anna was thirteen and quite helpful to the women. Their families had become close, and Maria was happy to have such good neighbors.

They had all decided to worship and celebrate Christmas together. Everyone gathered at the home of Christoph and Maria. They sang Lutheran hymns. They were all thankful that they had survived the journey to their new home, and they prayed for the families that had lost loved ones along the way. Karl had shot a duck down by the river, and the women prepared it for the meal. It was a wonderful time for all.

After Christmas, there was a big snowstorm. Since there were stairs leading down to their front door, Christoph had to shovel the snow every few hours to keep the door from being blocked. It was also more challenging to get to the barn the animals were in. They were down to one pig and one cow, as Christoph had slaughtered the other pig for meat. Some days it was all he could do to get the milk to the house without spilling it.

It was cold and snowy for the next two months, and then in March, it started to warm up. The snow melted on the sunny days, and there were puddles of standing water everywhere. The wind blew every day, and if there was any moisture, it came in the form of snow. Almost every day, Christoph and Maria were talking about the wide extremes of the weather. They were used to gradual changes, so these weather changes were going to make it difficult to determine when they would be able to plow the fields and sow the seeds.

By April, the snow had melted, so Christoph plowed the fields. The wind kept blowing every day, and as the soil dried out, the wind would blow it away. Igor had told Christoph and Karl that they needed to wait until May to plant because the overnight temperatures were still around freezing. About the time Christoph made headway plowing the rocky soil, it snowed. After the snow melted, the fields were too wet to do anything.

Christoph and Karl had to start over the next week once again plowing the fields. The soil was still quite rocky, even after multiple attempts to plow. The areas they had marked off for the vegetable gardens seemed to have better soil. The rest of the land was going to be challenging. What they didn't plow was set aside for cattle grazing. Christoph had one cow, but Karl had two.

By May, they thought it was safe to plant the vegetable gardens. They had seeds for lettuce, cabbage, and peas. They also had potatoes to plant. Everything had to be frost-resistant, as the mornings were still quite cool. By the end of the month, the garden was looking like it would produce; but then one afternoon, a strange storm happened. It started with lightning and thunder, and rain began to fall. Next, something happened that the settlers had never seen before. There were balls of ice falling out of the sky, and they were shredding the plants. Karl and Christoph dropped their plows and ran from the fields.

"What is happening?" shouted Christoph.

"I don't know. I've never seen anything like this," shouted Karl.

Maria panicked, convinced that they would never be able to grow food. After the storm ended, Lena, Hans, and Anna came over to check on Maria.

"I thought the roof of our hut was going to collapse from all the pounding," said Lena.

Hans was hit by several of the ice stones as he was trying to round up the animals and put them in the barn. "It was really quite painful," he said.

The next morning, Christoph walked up the hill to talk to Igor about the strange storm. Through Igor's limited German, Christoph found out that this was hail, and this kind of weather was quite common in the spring. That afternoon when Christoph was working in the fields with Karl, they started talking about the storm again. Karl had been in the village purchasing supplies, and he talked to some of the settlers from the southern areas of the German states. Apparently, this weather was quite common there, and it was believed that it was caused by the mountains. There were mountains west of Merkel. Christoph and Karl decided that they would start watching the weather over the mountains when they were in the fields.

Maria and Lena spent the morning cleaning up the mess in the vegetable gardens. They had no more seed, so they were going to have to salvage as many plants as possible.

A couple of weeks later, the fields started to dry up. Christoph and Karl were still trying to plow the fields and remove the rocks. They were starting to get desperate, as they knew that they would have no food or money if they didn't produce a crop. Fortunately, the vegetable gardens were starting to recover from the hailstorm. Everyone was watching the skies over the mountains, and if they looked threatening, the men came out of the fields and the animals were put in the barn.

Both Karl and Christoph had received seeds to plant rye. Igor had told them to plant the rye in August for harvest next year in late spring. They kept plowing the land through July, and finally in August, they planted the seeds. After that, the two families started storing food in their root cellars for winter. Christoph and Karl had decided they would hunt ducks and rabbit for fresh meat. Christoph had also decided to butcher their last pig, hoping to be able to purchase more farm animals with money made off the rye harvest next summer.

When the first snow arrived in October, the rye appeared to be well established with deep roots. By Christmas, the snow and cold had settled in. Christoph, Karl, and Hans went hunting as often as possible. Igor had helped Christoph make a bow with arrows to hunt. He found this more efficient than using the Jäger rifle he had used in the war. The gun scared all the other wildlife away when it was fired, so one had to hope that they had hit the target because there was nothing else to shoot. Soon Karl and Hans were also hunting with bow and arrows.

"Quiet! There's a duck over by the shore of the river," said Hans.

"Aim very carefully and we will have another duck for Christmas, just like last year," whispered Karl.

Hans carefully aimed and pulled the bow back. The arrow went straight into the middle of the duck.

"Great shot," said Christoph. They all laughed and went down to the shore to get their duck.

The two families celebrated their second Christmas together, thankful for their health and the friendship they had forged together. So far, the winter seemed to be milder than it had been the previous two years. For this, they were also thankful.

CHAPTER

5

Merkel, 1768

By March 1768, there was rumor of sickness in the village. It seemed to be common in the larger families.

There was a doctor, Dr. Lang, who arrived the previous summer. He lived in the village of Kratzke, which was near Merkel. The Müller family, who lived approximately half a mile from Karl's family, were the first to get sick. All of them had fever with body aches. When they started getting a rash and then coughing and vomiting, Dr. Lang knew that they likely would not survive. Christoph was in the village purchasing supplies when he ran across Dr. Lang.

"How's the Müller family doing?" he asked.

"Not good. They all have a typhus-like illness, and they are not faring well," replied the doctor.

"What can we do to help?"

"The best thing to do is stay away from them and pray. I suspect others will become sick as well. It's very hard to survive in this harsh climate. The winters are a lot colder than we are all used to."

Everyone in the Müller family died that spring. Two adults and three children were lost. There were several other families who lost one or two loved ones as well. The deaths served to bond the community together. A cemetery was established on some land on a hillside, and there was talk of building a church. Everyone in Merkel was of the Lutheran faith, so only one church was necessary. Johann Merkel, the first mayor of the colony, called for a meeting of the men in the village to plan the construction of the church. It was decided that work would begin after the harvest of the winter rye.

Unfortunately, the rye crop was minimal that summer. Many farmers blamed the small crop on the rocky soil. Christoph and Karl worked in the fields the entire month of June. They produced very little crop beyond what their families needed to survive the winter. They had little left over to sell for transport to Saratov by the Russians. Christoph received enough money to purchase one pig to butcher for the winter and more rye seed to add to the fields.

"This is the best we can do this year," Christoph told Karl.

"We will continue plowing and then reseed in the fall. That's the best we can do. The rest is in God's hands," replied Karl.

"Speaking of God, maybe tomorrow we should help the other men with the building of the church."

"Good idea. We could use a break from the fields."

The next day Christoph and Karl joined some of the other men in the village who were building a prayerhouse that would act as their church. They used logs that were leftover from the building of the *zemlyanka* huts around the village and installed two woodstoves for heat during the winter. As the men worked, they started discussing the need for a school as well.

Within two weeks, the prayerhouse was completed, and they began building the schoolhouse. Within a week, the schoolhouse was completed as well. As luck would have it, Dr. Lang had spent time as a Lutheran pastor and was willing to conduct Sunday services. By the end of July, the prayerhouse was full of worshiping settlers from Merkel.

Every Sunday, Christoph and Maria walked to the prayerhouse for Sunday services. It was nice to be able to go to church with people in their community. The women formed groups that gathered and sewed winter clothing for people in the village. The men continued to work in the fields, sowing more rye seed for next spring's crop. Also, the women started harvesting the remaining crops from the vegetable gardens for storage in the root cellars during the winter.

The snow came early that year in October. Fortunately, most of the settlers were nearly finished with their winter preparations. Igor had told Christoph and Karl that he suspected that winter would be early this year.

"The mornings are colder than usual, and it's not as warm during the day. I suspect winter will be early this year," he told them.

He was right. It snowed every week, and it was cold. It was so cold and snowy that the children could not go to school. They had started school in October and were there for three weeks before the school had to shut down. The Hoffmann's oldest girl, Ida, had offered to teach the children. She was unmarried and could read, so it was thought that she would be able to teach the children how to read. The prayerhouse was also closed, as no one was able to travel through the rough weather.

Karl, Lena, Hans, and Anna were able to get to Christoph and Maria's home for a Christmas Day celebration. It was a sunny day, which made it easier for Karl's family to travel through the snowbanks. Maria fixed rabbit stew. They prayed and sang hymns. It had been weeks since they had been able to get to church, so they were happy to be able to worship together. They thanked God for the blessings bestowed upon them and asked Him to keep them healthy through the harsh winter.

Spring came early in 1769, just as winter had the previous fall. The children went back to school for a couple of months before the summer fieldwork began. It was windy in March and April, with little snow. Best of all, there were no hailstorms.

There was a significant increase in yield of the rye at harvest. This winter, everyone would have plenty of rye flour to make bread. There was more for sale to the Russians in Saratov, so the settlers were able to buy more animals.

CHAPTER

6

Maria heard the door of their *zemlyanka* hut open. She thought that it was too early for Christoph to be in from the fields.

As she turned to see who was there, she screamed. The ugliest man she had ever seen slapped her across the room. He was yelling at her in some language she didn't understand and waving his arms everywhere. She told herself to get up and run, but she couldn't. He began kicking her, and when he kicked her in the head, she blacked out. The robber found the root cellar and stole food and supplies.

Later that afternoon, Christoph returned from the fields and found Maria.

"Oh, dear Lord! My sweet Maria, please wake up," he yelled. Crying, he held her in his arms and rocked her, believing her to be dead. She started to moan. He ran to put cool water on a washcloth and placed it on her forehead. She was badly bruised on her face, arms, and back. Moving caused a lot of pain, but he gently picked her up and placed her in their bed, covered her with blankets, and ran as fast as he could to get help.

He found Karl and Lena getting ready to sit down for dinner.

"Quick! I need help. Maria was attacked in our hut today. We need a doctor," yelled Christoph.

"I'll get Dr. Lang. Go help Christoph," Karl said to Lena.

Karl ran through the village, asking if anyone knew the whereabouts of Dr. Lang. He was told that he was at the prayerhouse, so he ran there. Dr. Lang was working on his Sunday sermon when Karl arrived. He jumped up, and they both ran to Dr. Lang's horse and wagon, which was outside the prayerhouse. They rode to Christoph's hut, and Dr. Lang ran inside. He found Maria in significant pain from her injuries and Christoph very distraught over the situation. Lena was praying as Karl sat down next to her and held her.

Dr. Lang did a thorough examination of her injuries and found only bruising and abrasions, no broken bones. He was very concerned about her head injuries, as Maria was unable to tell anyone what had happened.

"She needs rest, and she must not be left alone," he said.

"Anna and I will care for her while the men are in the fields," replied Lena.

"We will have Hans stay on the properties to help with the animals and gardens. He can also guard against this happening again, since he has become such a good shot with a rifle and bow and arrow while hunting," said Karl.

"This looks like the work of a robber," replied Dr. Lang. "There have been several attacks along the Astrakhan trail. Fortunately, no one has died yet, but these robbers are becoming more brazen."

"It would be almost impossible to find out who did this, since the robbers know where to hide in this hilly terrain," said Christoph.

"The robber must have taken something from here," said Karl.

Christoph and Karl began looking around the hut, but nothing was gone. Then they went into the root cellar and found food and supplies missing.

"Apparently, he was hungry," exclaimed Karl.

Christoph was outraged. "He nearly killed my wife because he was hungry!"

When they came out of the root cellar, Dr. Lang was sitting with Maria. Lena had gone to their hut to retrieve the food that she had prepared for dinner to share with everyone. Karl ran out of the hut after her. When he reached her, he told her that he didn't want her walking alone, day or night. The situation with the robbers had become too dangerous. Karl helped Lena carry the food to Christoph and Maria's hut. Maria could only drink some tea, as she was too exhausted to eat. Dr. Lang stayed the night to watch over Maria. Before they went to bed, Christoph and Dr. Lang prayed for Maria's survival and return to good health.

The next morning, Maria was feeling a bit better and was able to talk. Her face was swollen and bruised on one side. She said that the man entered their hut and struck her immediately. She understood nothing that he shouted at her, and he knocked her down and kicked her repeatedly until she passed out. Dr. Lang believed that there would be more robbers, as they likely felt that the settlers were vulnerable and it would be easy for the robbers to escape and hide in the gorges of the Karamysh River near Merkel and surrounding villages.

"Maybe we should have the mayor call a meeting to discuss the problem," said Christoph.

"Good idea," replied Dr. Lang. "Perhaps we can schedule the meeting to be held after church this Sunday. The women and children should not be left alone without protection. This way they can also attend the meeting."

When Dr. Lang left, he went to the mayor's office to schedule the meeting. Mayor Merkel told him that there had been other attacks, and he felt that something should be done.

After the attack, Anna stayed with Maria during the day. Maria spent very little time out of bed the first week. Hans was never far away, working with the animals and the gardens. He was also armed and ready to use the rifle, if necessary. Christoph and Karl continued working in the fields.

On Sunday, after the church service, the settlers held a meeting with the mayor to discuss solutions to the robber problem. Mayor Merkel had discussed the problem with the government office in Saratov and was told what the settlers could, and could not, do.

"We can defend ourselves, but if we capture a robber, we must turn them over to the Russian authorities. We cannot exercise punishment against robbers. If we capture someone, the Russians will transport him to Saratov," said the mayor. "We can build a jail to house the captured robbers while transport is being arranged," he added.

Some of the settlers wanted the right to punish the robbers, but they were reminded by the mayor of the oath of allegiance and the contract signed by each of them to adhere to the laws of Russia.

The settlers could not punish Russian citizens for crimes, only the Russians could. Finally, it was agreed that the men would build a jail to house any robbers caught and awaiting transport to Saratov by the Russians.

Anna nursed Maria back to health, and within three weeks, she was doing most of her work. The two families spent even more time together, feeling the need to protect each other. Even though the Russian government had found a solution for prosecution of any robbers who were captured by the settlers, they still had no way to stop the robbers from committing the crimes. Unfortunately, there were several settlers killed, and the problem increased when Gypsy bands started camping around Merkel a couple of years later.

CHAPTER
7

Merkel, 1774

On a warm spring morning, Karl and Christoph were walking to the fields when Karl mentioned the new people in the village.

"Did you hear about the gypsies that have come into the village?" he asked.

"I've heard that they have come into several of the villages. It might be time for the mayor to have another meeting," replied Christoph.

"Yes, perhaps our new pastor will allow us to meet after church on Sunday. Of course, I doubt that Pastor Gottlieb will be able to stay for the meeting since he has a church service in Kratzke after he finishes our service."

"How do you like this situation with the pastor performing services in four villages?" asked Christoph.

"I think it's harder on the pastor than us," laughed Karl.

"Well, Dietel village wanted the parish in their village, and none of us have a pastor available. So if Pastor Gottlieb wants to travel from Dietel to Merkel, and then to Kratzke and Kautz every Sunday to preach, then we should be thankful."

"I agree, and I think Dr. Lang agrees too. He is being run ragged just being a doctor. I have no idea how he fits preaching into his schedule," replied Karl.

Two weeks later, there was a meeting after church to discuss the gypsies. They had set up camps outside the village with the intention of staying there for the winter. Several of the settlers wondered what they were going to do for food during the cold winter. Others suggested that the village try to provide food to them; after all, that would be the Christian thing to do. "I agree," the mayor stated. "God has commanded us to take care of the poor." So several families decided to try this approach on the new visitors.

After the fall harvest, Maria and Lena fixed baskets of food for Christoph and Karl to take to the gypsy camp. The rye harvest had been better than ever that spring, and the women had made bread for them to take. They also added some fresh vegetables to the baskets. When Christoph and Karl delivered the baskets, the gypsies appeared to appreciate their kindness. Communication was challenging, as Karl and Christoph understood nothing that was being said. But they did notice something about some of the gypsies that was of concern: several people were coughing a lot.

"Did you notice all that coughing?" asked Karl as they were leaving.

"Yes, I did. Maybe the smoke from their fire pits is making them cough."

Even though the settlers tried to help the gypsies, many of them died during the harsh winter. When spring arrived, several of the gypsies left and headed north along the Volga River. There was talk that they were headed to Moscow. But there were several who stayed in the camp, and more arrived.

When the fields dried up in May of 1775, Christoph and Karl began the rye harvest.

"This looks like the best harvest we've ever had," said Christoph.

"Well, we've been at this for nine years. Maybe we've worked this soil enough to grow something here," replied Karl. They both laughed as they continued to work.

That summer was their best harvest since they had settled along the Volga River. The vegetable gardens produced the highest yield to date as well. Again, they shared some of their bounty with the gypsies. There had been reports of some of the gypsies robbing settlers, but Karl and Christoph's families had had no trouble. When Christoph and Karl delivered the food baskets to the gypsies, they noticed that almost all of them were coughing and some of them were too weak to walk. On the way back to their settlements, Karl said, "I hope they aren't sick with something. I'm worried."

"I am too," replied Christoph.

By Christmas, both Karl and Lena were coughing and were getting weaker by the day. Anna and Hans were trying to take care of their parents, but Hans had become overwhelmed by their illness and his need to take care of the animals. So Maria helped Anna care for them. Their health continued to worsen, and eventually, they began coughing up blood. Christoph went to get Dr. Lang who knew before he saw them what they had.

"Consumption," he said when he saw them. "It's all over the village."

"What can we do?" asked Christoph.

"Make them comfortable and pray."

"Karl and I noticed that the gypsies have been coughing when we delivered food baskets to them."

"I've heard that from several sick settlers, and that may be where this started," replied Dr. Lang.

Maria began to pray, "Our heavenly Father, we pray that you will deliver our dear friends and neighbors from this horrible illness. We can't lose them. We trust that you will heal them and heal others in our village with the same illness. In Jesus's name, we pray. Amen."

In April of 1776, Lena passed away. Within a week, Karl had also died. Hans and Anna fell into a state of hopelessness. Maria and Christoph did everything they could to help them cope. Many settlers died, and what gypsies who hadn't died moved on. The settlers were happy to see them leave. Many believed that the gypsies had brought this death upon them.

CHAPTER

As outlined in the manifesto of Empress Catherine II, inheritance law stated that the eldest son inherited the property upon the death of his father, so Hans inherited all the property belonging to Karl.

He was twenty-four and not married. He had a lot of responsibility thrown upon him. Thankfully, Christoph was of great help to him. Maria and Anna worked together tending the animals and the gardens. Anna, at age twenty-two, had learned a lot from her mother, but she appreciated Maria's help. It was a very difficult time for all, as Christoph and Maria had lost dear friends, and Hans and Anna had lost their parents.

Hans and Christoph worked together harvesting the rye in the spring and then spent the summer plowing the fields, just as Karl and Christoph had done for so many summers. This was also the summer that the first installment of repayment for the journey from Hamburg was due. Fortunately, Christoph and Karl had been setting aside money for this over the last few years, as Hans had just inherited his father's debt. Maria and Anna were preparing the vegetables for winter storage when Maria started coughing.

"Maria, you have been coughing for a week," Anna said one afternoon.

"Oh, it's nothing. Probably dust," replied Maria.

Anna wasn't so certain that it was just dust, so she spoke to Christoph about it. "Maria is starting to do a lot of coughing," she told him.

"I've heard it at night too, but she says it's nothing," he replied.

"I think we better watch her. This is how my parents sounded when they first got sick."

Maria's coughing worsened, and by Christmas, she was so weak that she could hardly get out of bed. Christoph was horrified. The thought of losing his wife was more than he could handle. Hans found Dr. Lang, and he came to see Maria.

"Even more people are sick than last year, and the gypsies are gone," he said. "Unfortunately, we still have no way to fight this, but there have been people who became sick and survived. Hopefully, Maria will get through this."

"We will pray and make her comfortable, just as we did with your parents," Christoph told Hans and Anna.

Within a couple of days, Maria started coughing up blood. At that point, Christoph knew the end was near. Two weeks later, Maria passed away. Those who were healthy attended her funeral. She was buried in the cemetery next to the prayerhouse. All Christoph had left was Hans and Anna. He and Maria were not able to have children, so there were no heirs if something were to happen to Christoph. Christoph was fifty-three, and even though Maria was ten years older than him, he never planned to lose her so soon.

It was prayer that sustained Christoph through that winter. While he had always attended church on Sunday when the weather allowed, he now prayed daily for strength and healing to help him cope with the death of his wife. He felt some guilt because he had put Maria through so much, both traveling to the Volga settlements and having to endure the harsh life in the settlements.

Pastor Gottlieb spent extra time with Christoph to help him work through his grief throughout the spring and summer. Christoph knew that he needed to be strong for Hans and Anna. While they were adults, they had still lost their parents at a young age and had a great deal of responsibility.

Once the fields dried up in the spring, Christoph and Hans began the rye harvest. With each passing day, they became a family. The men would work in the fields, and Anna would tend to the animals and gardens. She had also become a good cook, much to the delight of the men. On Sundays, they went to church together.

Several years earlier, Karl and Christoph had pooled some of their money together to purchase a horse and wagon that both families used. On Sundays, they put on their best clothes and rode in their wagon to church. Hans, who was quite handsome, had a female admirer at church, so he was eager to attend every week. Her name was Johanna, and there seemed to be a lot of talking and laughing when they were together.

Christoph was happy to see Hans enjoying himself. One Sunday after church, Johanna joined the three of them for Sunday dinner. Hans had shot a duck with his bow and arrow, and Anna fixed it, as she was taught by her mother and Maria, by roasting it over the open fire. The food and conversation were joyful. It had been a long time since Christoph, Hans, and Anna had been so happy. Johanna was a bright light in all their lives. Hans took Johanna home in the wagon, and when he returned, he told Christoph and Anna that he was going to marry Johanna.

"Did you propose to her?" asked Anna.

"Not yet, but I'm going to very soon," replied Hans.

"It's probably time for Anna to find a young man to marry as well," responded Christoph. Anna could not look at Christoph. Instead, she stared at the floor. She was interested in a man, but he wasn't young.

Christoph didn't know this, but Anna found herself attracted to him. He was fifty-three, but he didn't look old. He was strong and muscular, and most of his hair was still dark brown. Many men his age had white hair and looked beaten down by the hard life that the settlers endured. When he wasn't in the fields, she spent as much time with him as she could.

By Christmas 1778, Hans had proposed to Johanna, and they were going to get married in the spring. Anna's attraction to Christoph was becoming stronger by the day, and Christoph had figured out what was happening. The attraction was mutual, but Christoph struggled with their age difference. Something told him this wasn't right, but he knew what love felt like; and this was love.

That winter, Christoph and Anna spent a lot of time together. They decided that they would also get married in the spring. They talked to Hans and Johanna about having both weddings together. Then they presented the idea to Pastor Gottlieb.

"I'm not really surprised that this is happening," he laughed. "I'm so happy for all of you."

The wedding day was a bright, sunny day in June. Many in the village came to the double wedding and enjoyed the celebration afterward. There was food, singing, and dancing. It was a joyful time for all.

CHAPTER

9

Not much changed after the weddings. Christoph and Hans worked together in the fields, and Anna and Johanna harvested the gardens and put food up for storage for survival through the winter.

One morning in late fall, Anna was feeling a bit sick to her stomach. She had started feeling ill in the mornings. After a couple of weeks of this, she thought she knew what was wrong.

"Johanna, I think I might be pregnant," Anna said.

"That's so wonderful, Anna. Christoph will be so happy," replied Johanna.

"I don't want to tell him yet. I will go see Dr. Lang before I tell Christoph anything. If I'm not pregnant, he will be very disappointed, and I don't want to do that to him."

The next week, Anna went to the village to see Dr. Lang. She was indeed pregnant. Anna was so happy, and she planned to tell Christoph when he returned from the fields in the evening.

"My love, I have something to tell you. I saw Dr. Lang today, and we are going to have a baby," she said, barely able to hold back tears of joy. Christoph was speechless. This was wonderful news. He hugged her and kissed her. He never thought that this would happen. He and Maria were unable to have children, so to Christoph, this was truly a miracle.

Christmas of 1779 was a wonderful Christmas for both families. After so much tragedy with the deaths of Karl, Lena, and Maria, they felt blessed. Christoph and Anna were particularly joyful because of the future birth of their child.

In the spring of 1780, Anna gave birth to a son. Christoph was so happy and proud, as he finally had an heir. Because they knew this was a gift from God, they named him Christian.

That summer, Christian was baptized in the church. Anna and Christoph were completely captivated by their son. As soon as he could walk, he tried to follow his father outside. He loved the animals. He especially enjoyed chasing the chickens. It was almost impossible to work and keep track of him at the same time because he was so curious.

As Christian grew older, he went to the fields with the men. He was too young to do much besides watch; nevertheless, he loved being out there with his father. In fact, he spent so much time with his father that it was nearly impossible to get him to go to school. Christoph took Christian to school in the wagon and was there in the afternoon to pick him up. Christian loved the heavy snowstorms because then he could spend the day with his parents.

As Christian got older, he was more able to help the men in the fields. He also helped his mother with the animals and the vegetable gardens. He loved both of his parents dearly, but he was especially close to his father. When he grew up, he wanted to be just like him.

During the harvest in the spring of 1789, Christoph, Hans, and Christian were working in the fields when Christoph collapsed and fell to the ground. He wasn't moving as Hans and Christian ran to him.

"Father, Father, please wake up," Christian cried. Hans feared the worst as they loaded Christoph into the wagon. He wasn't moving; in fact, he wasn't breathing either.

They raced to Dr. Lang. "He has passed," Dr. Lang said, tears in his eyes.

Christian began crying. "No, no, no," he screamed. Hans tried to hug him, but Christian was inconsolable.

Dr. Lang went to find Pastor Gottlieb, and together they went to see Anna. "We have grave news for you, Anna," said Pastor Gottlieb.

"Christoph passed away in the fields this morning," Dr. Lang added. Anna was silent, stunned by what she had just heard.

"Where's Christian?" she finally asked.

"He is in my office with his father and Hans," replied Dr. Lang.

"Please take me there," she responded.

When they arrived, Christian ran to his mother and hugged her. When Anna saw Christoph lying in the bed in Dr. Lang's office, she wanted to fall on the floor and cry, but she knew that she had to be strong for her son. Christian was only nine and his father was his whole life, so Anna knew this was going to be very difficult for him.

"Could we have some time alone with him?" she asked.

"Sure. We will make the necessary arrangements," they replied.

"I'll wait outside," said Hans.

Anna and Christian sat holding each other, looking at Christoph. Anna held his cold hand. "Mother, how will we survive without father?" asked Christian.

"We will take care of each other for the rest of our lives, just as he would want us to," she replied. "God will take care of us. We must have faith."

Everyone in the village of Merkel and several people from the neighboring villages were at Christoph's funeral. Christoph had no enemies and was very well liked. This was evident given the number of people in attendance. The prayerhouse could not hold all the people, and many were standing in the yard during the service. Afterward, Christoph was buried next to Maria in the cemetery. Several of the women offered to be of help to Anna, and many of the men offered to help Hans in the fields. Christian had just inherited the farm at the age of nine, so he would need lots of help for several years to come.

CHAPTER

10

As Christian began to take over the farm, many times he felt like his father was with him. The land had become more productive, and with each passing year, the yield was much greater.

Christian had so much work to do that he abandoned school altogether. Hans not only helped Christian but also taught him everything he needed to know. Christian knew that no classroom could teach him how to farm. Hans and Johanna had given birth to two daughters, Catharina and Barbara. As they grew older, they helped their mother and Anna.

In 1796, the Russian crown demanded that the settlers pay taxes. They had been tax exempt during the entire time living in the settlements. Most of the original settlers were dead, and many of their heirs knew nothing of the taxation that would happen thirty years later. There was land on both farms that had been left to pasture by Christoph and Karl, and Hans and Christian decided that they would have to plow some of it to have more money to pay the taxes.

"This rocky soil is really hard to plow," said Christian.

Hans laughed at him and then told him about the Russian *sokhi* plows, which were wooden plows that Karl and Christoph used to plow the other fields.

"I guess I better stop complaining," replied Christian.

"Yes, you better since we have iron-tipped plows pulled by horses," laughed Hans. "We'll plow the land this summer and plant millet seeds in August for harvest next spring."

Since so many farmers were plowing more land for spring harvest, it was decided that the village needed a second grain storage magazine. So when Christian and Hans weren't plowing the fields, they were helping the other men build the grain storage magazine. Only ten percent of the stored grain was to be set aside for the settlers' use; the rest belonged to the Russian crown.

On Sundays, nearly everyone attended church in the summer. Christian had his eyes on a particular young lady named Sofia. Church was his opportunity to meet a girl who was not part of his family, as he spent the rest of the week working. He loved to go on walks with Sofia after church. Christian had decided that he wanted to marry Sofia, but they were both only sixteen. During one of their Sunday walks, he decided to ask her.

"Sofia, I love you so much. Will you be my wife?" he asked.

"I love you too, and I want to marry you. But I don't know if my parents will let me because I'm only sixteen," she replied.

"I will ask your father for your hand in marriage."

"How about we have you over for dinner next Sunday after church, and you can ask him then."

"Perfect," he replied.

The next day, Christian told Hans that he wanted to marry Sofia and that he was going to ask her father next Sunday.

"Have you talked to your mother?" asked Hans.

"Not yet," replied Christian.

"Well, you better talk to her before next Sunday. You are only sixteen, and she needs to know what you are thinking."

That evening, Christian spoke with his mother.

"I'm really not surprised," she replied.

"Mother, I really love her."

"I know you do, and I know she loves you. But don't be surprised if her father asks you both to wait a year or two because you are both only sixteen. Her father has the right to do this," she responded.

The next Sunday, Christian went to dinner at Sofia's house, and he asked her father for her hand in marriage. Just as his mother had said, Sofia's father asked that they wait one year before getting married. Christian and Sofia agreed to wait.

This gave Christian and Anna time to prepare for some changes in living arrangements. Christian and Hans built a cabin against the hillside that was larger than the *zemlyanka* hut that Christian and

Anna were currently living in. It was agreed that Anna would stay in the hut, and Christian and Sofia would move into the cabin after they were married.

Finally, Christian and Sofia were seventeen, and they were allowed to set the wedding date. They were married in the prayer-house on a warm, sunny day in late spring of 1797. The wedding was beautiful.

"You are absolutely gorgeous," Christian told Sofia. This was a new beginning for Christian. It had been eight years since the horrible day that his father had died, and he hoped to finally move on. He didn't have the strong faith in God that Sofia had, and he was hoping that this would now change.

The next week, Christian and Hans were harvesting rye and millet.

"I'd say marriage is treating you well," said Hans.

"It is. I've never been happier," replied Christian. "There has been a void in my life since my father died, and now Sofia has filled that void."

"That's wonderful to hear. You have been through a lot the last few years. You had to grow up too fast after losing your father. God was testing you, and now he has rewarded you with Sofia," replied Hans.

"I've never thought that God was testing me. I've felt like he has forsaken me," said Christian. "Sofia and I pray every night that I will regain my faith in God."

"Christian, don't feel that way. I had my doubts when your mother and I lost our parents. But I soon realized that I shouldn't be angry with God or afraid that he has rejected me, because he hasn't," replied Hans. "Turn to God and be patient and obedient."

That fall, Sofia started feeling sick in the morning. Anna knew exactly what was wrong. Dr. Lang had long ago stopped practicing, but he had trained a new doctor, Dr. Grass. Christian helped Sofia into the wagon so he could take her to see Dr. Grass. The news was very good. They were going to have a baby. They were so happy, and they could hardly wait to tell Anna and Sofia's parents.

The following summer, Sofia gave birth to a healthy baby boy. They named him Johann. Four years later, they had another baby boy, and they named him Jacob.

After Jacob was born, Hans and Christian were together in the fields. Hans had a question for Christian. "So do you feel that God has forsaken you now?" he asked.

"Not at all. I'm so blessed. I have a beautiful wife who has given me two sons," replied Christian.

"We are all blessed," responded Hans. "We have had several years of good harvest. There has been plenty of moisture with no signs of drought in the future."

"Have you seen the gypsies that are camping outside of town?" asked Christian.

"Yes, I have. The men in the village are worried about them being there. The last time they were here, several people, including my parents and your stepmother, died of consumption," replied Hans. "The gypsies were blamed for causing the sickness."

"I didn't know that."

"Your father never spoke of it. He took losing his first wife very hard."

"I think we all better keep a close eye on these gypsies," responded Christian.

CHAPTER
11

Merkel, 1813

As the number of gypsies camped outside the village increased, the anxiety of the settlers increased as well. They were afraid to be near the gypsy camps because so many settlers had died of "the sickness."

Some wondered where they were getting food, wood, or other essentials. Then it became obvious. They were stealing from the settlers. Several women were attacked, and their animals and food were stolen while the men were in the fields. Young boys were taught how to fire a rifle and protect their family.

Johann and Jacob were both old enough to help in the fields, but one of them always needed to be at home to protect the women. Finally, the men had enough of the behavior of the gypsies. The stealing and the violence had to stop. There was a meeting following church in which it was decided that the gypsies had to move on. The mayor and several other men had decided to meet with them and ask them to leave.

Later that week, they went to the gypsy camp and tried to convince them to leave. The gypsies refused to go. The following Sunday after church, the mayor met with the settlers and told them this. No one was surprised, and it was agreed that they would have to be forced out. Christian and several other men decided to form a militia whose job it would be to force the gypsies out of the area.

The militia conducted raids on the camps designed to scare the gypsies into leaving. They would ride their horses through the camp, firing their rifles into the air. Some of the gypsies left, but most stayed; and the violence between them and the settlers increased.

By the summer, the militia was conducting a raid nearly every night. The gypsies had stolen rifles, so they could now shoot back. The raids were now becoming more dangerous for the settlers, with several being injured or killed. Hans was in his sixties, so he was too old to participate; but Christian went on nearly every raid. On this night, the militia hoped to finally convince the gypsies that they needed to leave.

As the men rode their horses toward the gypsy camp, they were talking about how the gypsies had become such fierce fighters. As they approached the camp, there was gunfire. The horses became spooked. Christian's horse reared up and bucked him off, but his foot became stuck in the stirrup. The horse dragged him for several yards before he was able to free his foot from the stirrup. He tried to stand up, but he couldn't. The pain was intolerable. Finally, he was helped to safety, but he could not stand on his foot.

"Just take me home. I'll be fine in the morning," Christian told the men who were tending to him. They did as he asked.

Anna and Sofia spent the night trying to make him comfortable. The next day, Johann went to get Dr. Grass. Christian's foot was swollen and bruised badly. Even if he could stand on his foot, he couldn't put it in a boot.

"Looks like you probably broke your foot," said Dr. Grass after examining Christian's foot. "You need to rest and stay off of your foot so it can heal."

"How long will it take?" asked Christian.

"Hard to tell. Maybe a month."

Christian became irritated. "How am I going to farm?"

"Your boys will have to do it while you rest," responded Dr. Grass. When he went out the door, Dr. Grass told Sofia to keep him off his foot and said that he would be back the following week.

Johann and Jacob helped Hans in the fields, and Sofia did the best she could to keep Christian in bed, resting. She had help because the pain was so bad that Christian had no desire to stand on his foot. The swelling and bruising did not decrease, and Christian's foot did not look better when Dr. Grass came back to see it the next week.

"I'm surprised you are not getting better," the doctor stated. "Are you sure you are not walking on it?"

"I can't even put it on the floor, let alone walk on it," replied Christian. "It's horribly painful."

"I guess you will have to continue with bed rest, and I will be back next week."

A few days later, Sofia noticed that Christian's toes were turning black. When she touched them, he couldn't feel it. Within days, there was a foul-smelling liquid coming from his foot, and he was shivering in the middle of the July heat. Johann went to get Dr. Grass.

Dr. Grass was shocked to see the condition of Christian's foot. He had never seen anything like this. He had no idea why Christian was so sick when all he had done was break his foot. He had seen black toes on people with frostbite, and he knew that they would eventually fall off; but this was worse than that. "Make him as comfortable as possible," he said to Sofia. "I will be back tomorrow."

The next day when Dr. Grass returned, Christian was having trouble breathing and had sweaty, clammy skin. If he spoke, no one could understand what he was saying. Anna, Sofia, the boys, and Hans and Johanna were all praying at his bedside. Dr. Grass felt helpless. Christian was a young man, only thirty-three. He just couldn't understand how this could happen.

Within two days, Christian was gone. Everyone was devastated. Anna had lost her husband and now her son.

"No one wants to outlive their child," she said. Sofia and the boys were totally lost. Johann was fifteen, and Jacob was only eleven. They were now the men of the household. Hans was not a young man, but he knew that he would have to teach farming to Johann and Jacob, just as he had done for Christian.

The prayerhouse was full for Christian's funeral, just as was the case for his father. After Christian's injury and death, the men in the militia met with the mayor. It was decided to request help from the Russian government in Saratov in handling the problems with the gypsies. Anna was disappointed that the decision wasn't made before Christian's death. She wasn't coping with Christian's death and generally felt that God had abandoned her family.

Sofia was trying to cope with her own grief and her mother-in-law's lack of faith at the same time. She had to remain strong for her boys. She prayed morning and night for the strength to get through this.

By fall, Anna had started believing that she had no reason to live. Sofia became alarmed by this and contacted the new pastor, Pastor Vogt. He visited Anna and tried to convince her that God has a plan for her, and while this has been very painful for her, God will guide her through this painful time of her life.

"Why would God take my son from me?" she asked.

"Christian was needed in heaven," he replied. "God will take care of you."

Pastor Vogt came to visit Anna several more times before winter set in and limited everyone's travels. Sofia tried to get Anna to move into the cabin with them, but she refused. She ate less food, many days eating nothing at all. Johann and Jacob looked in on her daily, but most days she wouldn't even let them in the door of her hut.

One morning in February when the boys went to check on their grandmother, she didn't answer the door. They went inside and found her lying in bed. She didn't respond when they spoke to her. Johann touched her face, and it was ice-cold.

"Grandmother has passed," he told Jacob. Both had tears running down their faces when they told their mother. Sofia couldn't believe this could happen.

"Johann, go get Hans. We need to get Dr. Grass out here."

"Yes, Mother," he replied as he ran out the door.

Dr. Grass felt that Anna had lost her will to live.

"Her loss was too great," he said. "There have been many settlers over the years who have not been able to cope with the harshness of this life. Some have even taken their own lives."

"Anna was one of the few original settlers left," replied Hans. "Now Johanna and I are among the few remaining, and we were children when we were brought here by our parents."

"I guess it's hard for me to understand this because I know no life beyond here," responded Sofia. "My grandparents and parents left Germany because of religious persecution and endless wars. These are two things that we have not had to deal with here."

"Life has gotten better here over the decades," replied Hans.

"Well, we have another funeral to arrange," sighed Sofia.

"Johann and Jacob, let's go find Pastor Vogt," responded Hans.

<h1 style="text-align:center">CHAPTER
12</h1>

After Anna's funeral, it was time to start preparing for the work in the fields.

Johann was the heir, so the family farm was his. He had a lot to learn. Jacob wondered where he would farm when the time came for him to marry and move away from his mother. Hans told him not to worry about that and to focus on learning farming.

Hans and Johanna had two daughters, so he had no heirs, since the oldest son was the heir to property. However, the inheritance laws made it possible for Hans to assign inheritance to another relative. Jacob was his sister's grandson, so he could inherit Hans's property. Hans decided to not tell this to Jacob just yet.

Over the next few years, the two families continued to work together managing the farms. Hans was nearly seventy years old and starting to slow down. Johann and Jacob were becoming stronger and able to do almost all the work. Besides, Hans had two daughters to marry off. Catharina and Barbara married within a year of each other. Hans and Johanna were proud parents, but the marriage of his daughters forced Hans to finally name the heir to his property.

Jacob was stunned. "Are you sure about this?" he asked Hans.

"I'm positive. I know that you and your brother will work together to keep both farms going," said Hans. "When I die, you will inherit this property. Until then, you will have to help me because I'm getting up there in years, and I can't handle all the work."

"You can count on me and my brother," responded Jacob.

As time went on, it became more obvious to the boys that Hans was slowing down. Sofia noticed the same with Johanna. It was rare for a settler to live into their seventies, so when Hans passed away in his sleep, no one was surprised. He had turned seventy the month before. Johanna went to live with her daughter Catharina, leaving the farm vacant. The following spring, Jacob received word that the farm was now his, as Johanna had passed away as well.

Sofia had started hosting weekly prayer meetings in her cabin after Anna died. She took to heart the things that Dr. Grass had said about the harshness of life along the Volga River. She felt that through God, she had something to offer to her friends and neighbors. They would talk about the hardships and pray for strength and compassion.

One of the women who attended had recently lost her husband. Her name was Ella, and she brought her daughter, Elisabeth, with her to the prayer meetings. Johann and Jacob attended the meetings as well. Elisabeth and Johann were the same age, and they immediately took a liking to each other. Their courtship reminded Sofia of herself and Christian. She knew that eventually her son would want to marry Elisabeth.

A couple of months later, at the beginning of the meeting, Johann announced to the group that he and Elisabeth wanted to marry. Ella and Sofia were thrilled. "Looks like we have a wedding to plan," said Ella.

"And I can't think of any two women better than us to do it," added Sofia.

The wedding was beautiful. Johann and Elisabeth were so happy. They moved into the cabin, and Sofia went to live with Jacob. Together, Johann and Jacob managed both farms. They were quite successful, as were most of the farmers in the region. It had been years since they had seen drought. Most of the farmers felt that they had finally mastered the land. The population was increasing as well. In fact, on most Sundays it was impossible to get everyone in the prayerhouse for Sunday service. It was decided to raise money to build a new church. Pledges were secured from parishioners, and once there was enough money pledged, the men began building the new church.

A couple of years after they got married, Johann and Elisabeth had a son, whom they named Georg. The pregnancy had been difficult for Elisabeth. She spent the last four months in bed. Both Elisabeth and Johann were happy to have a healthy boy.

Johann and Jacob helped the other men build the new church when they weren't working in the fields. By the spring of 1826, the church was finished, just in time for Easter Sunday. Even though the sanctuary was much larger than the prayer house, it was completely full. Nearly everyone in Merkel was there. Paster Vogt was stunned by the attendance. It was a beautiful, sunny day, which was rare, as it was common for it to rain or snow on Easter.

The following year, Elisabeth gave birth to a second son. Her pregnancy went much better this time. This son was named Daniel. Elisabeth was thankful to have Sofia helping her with the boys. She had moved back in with Johann and Elisabeth when Jacob married after Georg was born. Having her living with them made it possible for Elisabeth to tend to the animals and gardens outside without worrying about two very active boys. Besides, Sofia was starting to slow down and found it more and more difficult to do the outdoor work. Most days, she was tired and was limited in the amount of work she could do around the house. "Mother, I'm concerned about you," said Johann. "You are tired all the time. Maybe you should see Dr. Grass."

"That's not necessary," she replied. "The same thing happened to my father when he was in his fifties. Perhaps God is preparing my place in heaven."

Then on a Sunday morning, Sofia did not join the family for breakfast. This had been the case a few mornings recently, but never on Sunday. Sofia rarely missed church.

Elisabeth knocked on Sofia's bedroom door. "Sofia, are you awake?" There was no answer. Elisabeth knocked again then entered the room. Sofia was lying in bed. She looked very peaceful. Elisabeth touched her hand: it was ice-cold. "Johann, come in here," she shouted.

Johann knew, as he approached the bed, that his mother was gone. The boys appeared in the doorway, but Johann didn't want them to see this. "Georg, take Daniel and go over to your Uncle Jacob's house. Tell him that he needs to come over here quickly."

The boys left to get Jacob. When Jacob arrived, he couldn't believe what he was seeing. "She was only fifty," he said.

"She hasn't been feeling well," replied Elisabeth.

"And she refused to see Dr. Grass," added Johann.

Georg and Daniel had moved their way into the room and were staring at their grandmother. "Is grandmother asleep?" asked Georg.

Johann turned toward his sons and kneeled in front of them. "No, grandmother has gone to be with the angels in heaven," he said. Both boys began to cry, and Elisabeth came over to hug them.

"We will have to talk to Pastor Vogt about the funeral," said Jacob.

"Sofia would want us to go to church this morning," replied Elisabeth.

"This is true," agreed Johann. "Let's go to church and talk to Pastor Vogt after the service."

The church was full for Sofia's funeral. She had been a model of faith for so many people through her prayer meetings. Many felt that she would be a great loss to the community.

Johann and Jacob were told by several that this was God's will, but they still found it hard to accept the loss of their mother. They were teenage boys when they lost their father, and now they were young men and had lost their mother. They were tempted to lose faith in God; but they knew that it was their mother's faith that got her through the death of their father, and that she would expect them to keep the faith with her passing.

CHAPTER

13

As time passed, Johann became more accepting of his mother's death. He found that work helped to clear his mind, and he certainly had enough work to do.

Georg was beginning to be of some help in the fields, and Daniel helped his mother with the animals and gardens. Elisabeth was once again pregnant, and almost three years after his mother's death, a baby girl was born. She was the first girl born to the family in Russia. They named her Emma.

The boys loved to play with Emma when they came in from their work. She was spoiled. When she started walking, she went to the vegetable gardens with Elisabeth, while the boys tended to the animals and worked in the fields. The work began to be taxing for Georg as he got older. He was quite thin, and his parents thought that maybe he wasn't eating enough. Fortunately, the yield in the fields, gardens, and animals was good, so there was plenty of food. No matter how much George ate, he was not putting on weight. Furthermore, they always had to carry extra drinking water to the fields because he was always thirsty. Both boys were teenagers, and Daniel was becoming strong; but George seemed to get weaker.

Finally, Johann and Elisabeth decided that Georg needed to see Dr. Grass. "I'm tired all the time," Georg told the doctor. "Some days, I don't even want to get out of bed."

"I think you need rest," Dr. Grass said. "Stay out of the fields for a month. Don't push yourself," he added.

"Is this the same illness my mother had?" asked Johann as Dr. Grass was leaving.

"I don't know. I've seen cases like your mothers in adults, but not kids," replied Dr. Grass.

Georg was forced to stay indoors and help his mother and sister when he was able. Rather than get stronger, he continued to get weaker. He slept most of the time. Dr. Grass returned after a month and couldn't believe what he was seeing. Georg was eighteen and should be a strong young man, but instead he was frail, weak, and barely able to walk. "I have no answers for you. I just can't explain what is causing this," the doctor told Johann and Elisabeth.

"What can we do?" asked Elisabeth.

"I suggest you get Pastor Vogt over here," he replied.

When Pastor Vogt arrived, Elisabeth was inside praying for her son. Johann was angry and met Pastor Vogt outside. Pastor Vogt knew that Johann had struggled with his faith since his mother's death ten years earlier. It was not uncommon for him to work in the fields rather than come to church on Sunday. No one in the family had been to church since Georg had become too weak to go.

"God has forsaken my family. First, it was my father. Then my mother, and she prayed all the time. Now it's my son. He is my heir. He can't die," shouted Johann.

"We cannot defy God's sovereign will," Pastor Vogt replied.

"He can't die," Johann cried as he fell to the ground.

Daniel came outside to help his father get up. "Father, we need to be strong for Georg, Emma, and Mother."

Pastor Vogt went inside to find Elisabeth and Emma praying at Georg's bedside. Georg was still breathing but could not be aroused. Daniel and Pastor Vogt joined them, and they prayed all night. At dawn, Georg stopped breathing. "God has taken him," said Pastor Vogt.

As they all left the room, they found Johann on the porch, crying. Nothing needed to be said. He knew that his eldest son was gone. He and Elisabeth held each other and wept.

As word spread through the village about Georg's death, people were shocked. How could a young man wither away and die? Could this sickness be spreading through the village?

After Georg's funeral, Elisabeth prayed daily that Daniel and Emma would remain well. Elisabeth took her children to church every Sunday, but Johann refused to go with them. One Sunday, Pastor Vogt spoke with Elisabeth.

"Johann is horribly hurt by the death of Georg," she said. "He blames God."

"I will speak with him," replied Pastor Vogt.

"Would you like to come to Sunday dinner this afternoon?"

"That would be wonderful. I'll talk to him then," he replied.

That afternoon, Pastor Vogt came to dinner and had a talk afterward with Johann.

"Let's go outside and talk," he said to Johann. "I know that the loss of your son has been too great, and you feel like God is not here. God is testing you, just as he has tested others here. This land where our ancestors settled seventy-five years ago is a harsh land. Many families have suffered severe losses. Your family is no different. You are no different, Johann. Everyone has had struggles here."

"I know, but I can't move beyond losing Georg," Johann replied.

"I will visit when I can, and we will pray," said Pastor Vogt. "And I want to see you in church with your family next Sunday."

Johann nodded his head to indicate that he would be there.

The following Sunday, Johann went to church with Elisabeth, Daniel, and Emma. After singing some hymns, Pastor Vogt began his sermon. "The scripture for today comes from Matthew 5 verses 3 through 12," he said.

> Blessed are the poor in spirit: for theirs is the kingdom of heaven. Blessed are they that mourn: for they shall be comforted. Blessed are the meek: for they shall inherit the earth. Blessed are they which do hunger and thirst after righteousness: for they shall be filled. Blessed are the merciful: for they shall obtain mercy. Blessed are the pure in heart: for they shall see God. Blessed are the peacemakers: for they shall be the children of God. Blessed are they which are persecuted for righteousness' sake: for theirs is the kingdom of heaven. Blessed are ye, when men shall revile

you, and persecute you, and shall say all manner
of evil against you falsely, for my sake. Rejoice,
and be exceedingly glad: for great is your reward
in heaven: for so persecuted they the prophets
which were before you. (Matthew 5:3–12)

"So what does this mean?" he asked. "In general, it means that God blesses those who mourn, are humble, are merciful. He blesses those who are poor, those who hunger for justice, and those who work for peace. And he blesses those with pure hearts and those who are persecuted for doing right.

"These are the beatitudes, and they are part of the Sermon on the Mount given by Jesus. Each beatitude tells how to be blessed by God. They do not promise wealth or pleasure, but being blessed by God means experiencing hope and happiness, regardless of life's circumstances. We have all faced challenges living here along the Volga River: failed crops, sickness, loss of loved ones. But in Jesus, we have hope, and that hope brings happiness."

As Pastor Vogt continued, tears began to form in Johann's eyes. "The kingdom of heaven is organized differently than what's seen on earth. Power and wealth are unimportant. We once again see our loved ones who have passed," he said looking at Johann. "No one is sick, and crops don't fail," he added. "Perhaps the most important quality needed is humility. We need to recognize our need for God. For some, this is a change in attitude." Johann began to weep as he realized how much he needed God in his life.

As he concluded the service, Pastor Vogt led them in prayer. "Lord, help us to remember what Jesus taught us. That he taught us that devotion to God and service to others is most important. Help us to remember our need for you, Lord God, as we leave worship today. Amen."

After hearing this, Johann started praying with his family; and just as his grandfather Christoph had done after losing Maria, he eventually regained his faith in God. Johann focused on his wife and remaining children. Daniel was now his heir, and it was important that he be ready to take over the farm when the time came.

Daniel had a strong faith, thanks to his mother. He went to church every Sunday with his mother and sister. He was also drawn to church by the pastor's daughter, Eva. Johann and Elisabeth knew where this was going, so Johann decided it was time to dig up the old *zemlyanka* hut and build a cabin for Daniel and his family to eventually live in.

Johann and Daniel spent most of the summer, after they finished plowing, removing the hut and building the cabin. The outside was finished just before the first snow. It was decided that the inside could be finished in the spring. Daniel was very excited, as he now felt he could propose to Eva.

The following Sunday after church, Daniel and Eva went on a walk. "Eva, I love you," he said. "Will you marry me?"

"I thought you would never ask," she replied.

Daniel and Eva got married the following spring. Within a month, Eva was pregnant with the baby due in March. Eva spent the summer and fall working with Elisabeth and Emma in the gardens, putting up food for the winter. By late fall, there were days when Eva needed to rest. As the snow started falling, she rested every day. Elisabeth was concerned, but it was impossible to get Dr. Grass out to the farm, as the snow was too deep for travel.

After Christmas, Eva started having contractions. Everyone knew that it was too early for the baby to be born.

"It's too early," Eva cried between contractions. Elisabeth prayed and got ready to deliver a baby. The baby girl was tiny, about the size of Daniel's hand. She moved and whimpered, but she didn't cry.

"She's so tiny," said Daniel.

"We need to keep her wrapped in blankets," Elisabeth told Daniel and Eva.

"She was born too soon," cried Eva.

"We must pray that she survives," said Daniel.

They named her Maria. Pastor Vogt was able to get to the cabin to baptize her the next day. Maria seemed to be doing well for about a week, but then she suddenly stopped feeding. The next morning, she was dead. Daniel and Eva were devastated. Pastor Vogt once again traveled through the snow to the cabin, this time to pray for his granddaughter.

When he arrived, he led them in prayer. "Father God, we have lost another precious life today. An innocent, tiny girl has left us to spend eternity with you. Please give us the strength to cope with this and thank you for the blessings you have granted to us. In Jesus's name, we pray. Amen."

"Family and faith will deliver us through this tragic loss," Daniel said to Eva as he held her.

By late summer, Eva was pregnant again. Dr. Grass insisted that she not work too much through the fall, as she had done the previous year. She had none of the symptoms that she had had with her first pregnancy, and in June, she delivered a healthy baby boy. Daniel wanted to name him after his older brother, so he was named Georg. Two years later, they had another baby girl, whom they named Catherine. Then Heinrich and Friedrich were born, also two years apart.

Daniel was happy to have the boys so that he would have plenty of help on the farm. Johann was starting to slow down, so as soon as Daniel could get Georg in the fields, he had him out there working with him so that his father wouldn't have to work so hard. Uncle Jacob was also starting to slow down, but he had a daughter, so there was no additional help in the fields.

CHAPTER
14

Merkel, 1861

In spring, word spread that Tsar Alexander II had emancipated the serfs in Russia. One evening, the men in Merkel met in the prayerhouse with the mayor to find out what this meant.

"Apparently, a system of self-government will be put into place throughout Russia, but this changes nothing for us," said the mayor.

"For now," responded Johann.

"We will be next, for sure. They have wanted to change our lives for years," added Jacob.

"All I know is that the codex of the colonists, as laid out in 1842, still applies to us," said the mayor. "We will continue our self-governance." The men were worried about what would come next, but there was nothing they could do for now.

On their way home, Jacob told Johann that he was going to name Daniel, heir to his property. "I have no son, so I need to name a relative. Just as Hans was my uncle, I'm Daniel's uncle. So I want him to be my heir," he said.

"Well, he is farming my land and your land right now," replied Johann.

"And he has three sons who will need cabins when they marry", added Jacob.

"I doubt we will be here for that. I'm sure that God will call us home by then," responded Johann.

After the meeting with the mayor, Johann and Jacob gave the situation with the serfs very little thought. They tried to help Daniel with the farming but were getting too old to do much. On a morning in June when they were harvesting the rye, Johann collapsed and fell into the field. Daniel ran to him, but Johann wasn't moving. Jacob got to him as quickly as he could.

"Father, father," Daniel shouted. There was no response. "We need to load him in the wagon and take him to Dr. Grass," shouted Daniel. They hurried into the village as fast as they could. While Jacob didn't say anything, he knew his brother had passed.

When they reached Dr. Grass's office, Johann's death was confirmed. Daniel was in shock. "How could he just fall over and die like that," he cried.

"The same thing happened to your great-grandfather Christoph," replied Jacob. "They both died doing what they enjoyed."

When they arrived home, Daniel had the task of telling his mother. She sat down and cried, but when she finally composed herself, she told them that Johann had been complaining of headaches for several weeks. She then told Jacob that he should stay with her for now. He had lost his wife a few years ago and she didn't think that he should be alone right now.

After Johann's funeral, Jacob went back to his cabin. Elisabeth and Daniel didn't know if this was a good idea, but Jacob insisted. He still helped Daniel in the fields and ate meals with the family, but it was obvious that he really missed his brother.

"It's like he is just going through the motions. He's lost," Daniel told his mother.

"We need to let him grieve," replied Elisabeth.

A couple of weeks later, Jacob didn't come by in the morning to go to the fields with Daniel and Georg. Daniel was worried, so they went to his cabin. "Stay outside," he told Georg. Daniel went inside and found Jacob lying in bed. His hands and face were cold to the touch. Daniel ran out of the cabin and told Georg to go get his grandmother.

Georg drove the wagon back to the cabin. "Grandmother, Father says you need to come to Uncle Jacob's cabin," shouted Georg as he ran into her cabin.

"What?" she asked.

"Quick, something has happened to Uncle Jacob," he responded. Georg took Elisabeth to Jacob's cabin.

When she went inside, she could already smell death. She knelt at Jacob's bedside, asking, "Oh, Lord, how many more of us will die here?" When she stood up, Daniel hugged his mother.

After Jacob's funeral, Elisabeth gave the papers to Daniel that pronounced him as Jacob's heir. Daniel now had two farms. "Good thing I have three boys," he said.

For the next eight years, Daniel and his boys farmed their land, and on Sundays, they thanked God for all their blessings. Their family had been farming for over one hundred years, and the land was quite fertile as a result. They had much to be thankful for. Then everything changed.

CHAPTER
15

The men of Merkel were to meet at the prayerhouse on Wednesday evening. They were told that Tsar Alexander II had made a decree that affected the Germans living along the Volga River. Everyone wondered what this could be about. Some were worried.

During the meeting, the mayor told the men that the codex of the colonists was discontinued, and many of the special privileges that they had been given were abolished. They now had the same status as the freed serfs. By the decree, the Volga Germans no longer had the right to self-government. Thus, they were now subject to the same bureaucratic provincial administration imposed on the Russian peasants.

"What does this mean?" asked Daniel.

"For starters, I'm no longer your mayor," replied the mayor. "The Russians will be governing us." This caused an angry roar in the room. Many wondered how this could happen, as the settlers had long ago been promised self-government forever. The men left vowing to not let the Russians take away their way of life. They had worked hard to survive—and in some cases, prosper—and no one was taking it from them.

Georg had gone to the meeting with Daniel. He was now sixteen and doing more of the work on the farm. "Father, what does this mean?" he asked.

"It's hard to tell right now," replied Daniel. "Your great-great-grandparents came here from Germany over one hundred years ago. They were promised land to farm, freedom of religion, and exemption from military service. So they traveled from Germany for hope of a better life. Now it looks like all of that may go away. We will have to wait and see how this all turns out."

Six weeks later, the men gathered again at the prayerhouse for another meeting. This time it was led by representatives of the Russian government. They spoke only Russian. Very few at the meeting were fluent in Russian. Daniel and Georg sat in their chairs, stunned. How were they to understand what was going on?

Fortunately, the now-former mayor was at the meeting, and after the government representatives left, he translated what was said. "First, all communications with the government will now be required to be in Russian. No more German. They want us to assimilate into Russian society. We can't be our own little German community anymore. Finally, Tsar Alexander II has passed a law allowing us to leave Russia if we want. This window of emigration will last for ten years."

One of the men shouted, "How are we supposed to learn Russian?"

"Maybe our mayor can teach us," responded Daniel.

"I could," replied the former mayor. "Maybe we can arrange something at the schoolhouse."

On the way home, Georg told his father how he felt about all of this. "Father, I don't like this. I don't think we should have to learn Russian. Maybe we should emigrate."

"I don't think we need to plan to leave. We only need to learn enough Russian to deal with the government," replied Daniel.

Over the next few months, those who were fluent in Russian held classes in the schoolhouse to teach Russian. Many refused to attend. They felt that they were being pushed to "Russify" and that this threatened their cultural identity. They were angered by the possibility of losing their language and culture.

By this time, Pastor's Vogt's son, Ludwig, had become pastor of the church. There was great concern that the next right that would be taken was their right to their religion. While none of the settlers could remember a time when they could not worship in their Lutheran faith, they had all heard stories of their ancestors leaving Germany because of religious persecution.

Soon prayer groups formed meetings in homes. Everyone prayed for the way of life that had been established throughout the generations. Pastor Vogt traveled from home-to-home praying with families.

For a couple of years, there was no word from the Russian government. Everyone stopped believing that their way of life was threatened. In fact, no one was any longer learning Russian. Then another meeting was announced. Again, it was held at the prayer-house. Daniel took Georg and Heinrich with him this time. It was announced that land ownership would be prohibited unless they converted to the Russian Orthodox faith.

After the Russian representative left, those who knew enough Russian translated for the rest. The room erupted in shouting. Not only was their religious freedom attacked but the promise of land ownership given to their ancestors by Catherine the Great was also gone.

Daniel took his boys home and gathered Eva; his daughter, Catherine; and his youngest son, Friedrich, for a family meeting. "We need to discuss something very important," he said. "The Russian government will not let us continue to own our land unless we convert to the Russian Orthodox religion."

"This can't be," replied Eva.

"It is, Mother," responded Georg.

"We will all think about this and continue to discuss it," said Daniel. "Our sons are our heirs, and the question is whether they will have land to own in their inheritance or whether they will rent and work the land. I will talk to my mother about this tomorrow."

Daniel's mother, Elisabeth, was now in her early seventies and had become quite frail. Some days she was too tired to help the other women, and she just stayed in her cabin. Daniel knew that when he talked to her about the meeting the previous evening, he would have to take care not to upset her. "Mother, there was another meeting last night with the Russians. They told us that we could not own our land unless we converted to the Russian Orthodox religion."

Elisabeth sighed and asked, "What is this religion?"

"I don't know, exactly," he replied. "All I know is that everyone was very upset last night after they found out about it."

"What are we going to do?"

"We are going to think about it. We have a lot to consider, as this affects the boys' inheritance," he replied.

"Daniel, what we need to do is pray and let God guide us to the correct answer," responded Elisabeth.

"You are right, Mother. We will pray tonight after dinner as a family, and we will continue to do so every night until we have an answer," he said.

It didn't take the family long to decide that they would not be leaving their Lutheran faith. In fact, no one in Merkel did. The entire village decided that the Russians could have their land. It became a joke that the Russians could have the land, but farming it was another story, as they didn't have a clue as to how to farm. The Russians decided that the settlers could retain ownership of their homes, belongings, barns, and animals. Daniel's family knew that eventually they would have to emigrate. But right now, his mother was too old and frail to travel to a new country.

In the spring of 1874, there was another meeting scheduled with the Russian representatives in the prayerhouse. This time, the exemption from military service was stripped from the settlers. It was announced that a new military law would go into effect immediately. It would require that all medically fit male Russian subjects, including the Germans who were now Russian subjects, to serve in the Russian army for six years when they reached the age of twenty.

Daniel turned to Georg, who was now nineteen. "No, Father, this can't be happening," said Georg.

"It's not going to happen," replied Daniel.

When Daniel and his sons returned home that evening, they told Eva about the meeting. She burst into tears. "All my sons will die in war," she cried.

"None of our sons will die in war," replied Daniel as he comforted her.

Daniel's mother, who was now too sick to stay alone, came out of her room. "Daniel's great-grandfather, Christoph, was the last in our family to serve in the military during war in Germany. He immigrated to this country so that no one in this family would ever serve in the military again."

"Yes, we were promised that we would be free from military conscription forever," added Daniel. "Our sons will not serve in the Russian military. We will find a way out of this. I don't even know how they would know who's twenty years old."

16

1874

Little did Daniel know, the Russians already knew how they would find out who was of age to serve in the military. They paid a visit to Pastor Vogt and demanded to see the parish records. "We want to see all of them," they demanded.

"Whatever for?" asked Pastor Vogt.

"That's the business of the Russian government, not yours." The Russians made a list from the baptismal records of all men who were of age. In addition to the young men who were twenty, the names of their fathers and younger brothers were listed. Georg was listed as eligible for military conscription the next year in 1875, with Daniel listed as his father. Heinrich and Friedrich were listed as younger brothers.

The next Sunday, Pastor Vogt gathered the men in the congregation for a meeting after church. "The Russians were here a few days ago," he stated. "They made a list from the baptismal records of all the men who are of age to be conscripted into the military. They also listed the names of their fathers and younger brothers."

At this point, everyone knew that this was serious. At home that afternoon, Daniel's family discussed emigration. The question was not whether they should emigrate but how and where they should go. There was also the question of whether Daniel's mother could make the trip.

Within a couple of weeks, word came around that there was a meeting scheduled in the neighboring village of Balzer. Daniel loaded everyone into the family wagon for the trip to Balzer. There were hundreds of people there. There were two men from Balzer who had decided that scouts should be sent to America to determine whether the country was suitable for resettlement. By the end of the meeting, nine men were selected to be scouts. None of the scouts were from Merkel, but they promised to deliver a report upon their return.

On the way home, Georg had some questions for his father. "Do you think the scouts will return?"

"I do, but I have no idea how long they will be gone," replied Daniel.

In June 1874, the scouts went to Saratov and boarded a train to Moscow. They knew that this trip would be different than the one made by their ancestors. None of them had ever seen a train, much less ridden on one. From Moscow, they took a train to St. Petersburg. From there, they traveled on a steamship to Hamburg.

After a couple of days in Hamburg, they boarded the steamship *Schiller*, which was owned by the German Transatlantic Steam Navigation Line. They arrived in New York in July, six weeks after they had left Saratov. After disembarking at Castle Garden, the New York immigration station, they met with officials from the German Lutheran Immigrant Mission stationed there.

They spoke to the scouts in German, but it was a struggle to communicate, as the scouts spoke a German language that had some Russian words mixed in. The officials from the mission took great interest in the scouts, and they recommended that they take a train to Kansas City, where they would find plenty of land to farm. So the scouts boarded a train to travel west and seek out land for farming.

The trip turned out to be challenging. The scouts spoke no English and very few Americans spoke German, so it was nearly impossible to ask questions. When they returned to New York, they once again met with officials from the Lutheran Immigrant Mission. This time they were told about the Homestead Act of 1862. They were told that if they intended to become citizens, then they could receive 160 acres of federal land if they agreed to farm the land.

The scouts had not been that impressed with America, but this caused them to wonder if this was the country for them to come to. They had been told that they would have the freedom to worship as they pleased, and they were told that there would be no forced military conscription, as the country was still recovering from their Civil War. The scouts boarded a steamship to Hamburg, thinking that they would have a favorable report upon arriving home.

The scouts held another meeting in Balzer after arriving home in October. The people in the villages were so happy that they returned safely. They had been praying for safe travel and return. Everyone was ready for a celebration when they returned.

The scouts, however, were quite serious about the information that they had gathered. They told everyone about the trip and the promise of land to farm and freedom of religion. But they also told them about the language problems, the unpopulated countryside, and sandy soil conditions. "Our ancestors did not speak Russian, and this soil was almost too rocky to farm. It took decades to work the soil to its current yield," responded Daniel.

Daniel's greatest concern was whether his mother could make the long trip. His daughter Catherine had stayed with her grandmother, while the others went to the meeting. When they arrived home, the family held a meeting discussing what they had heard. "Mother, do you think you could make a trip like this?" asked Daniel.

"If I'm supposed to survive this trip, God will take me there," she replied.

"I'm starting to get nervous about being drafted into the military. I'll be twenty next June," said Georg.

"It's been six months since we were told about the forced conscription into the military, and no twenty-year-old boys have been called up yet. We will have to wait and see when they are called up," replied Daniel.

"This trip will cost money. Where will we get it?" asked Eva.

"We will have to figure that out when the time comes," responded Daniel. "We can't go anywhere right now anyway. We must prepare for the coming winter."

CHAPTER
17

1875

The following spring, Pastor Schultz from the Immigrant Mission at Castle Garden traveled to Russia to visit the Protestant German colonies along the Volga River.

The first Sunday he was in Merkel, Pastor Vogt introduced him to the congregation. "Hello, I'm here to preach and to meet with families who wish to emigrate to America," he said.

After the service, Daniel spoke with Pastor Schultz. "I want to invite you to my home when you are available and discuss emigrating to America."

"How about later this week?" replied Pastor Schultz.

"Wonderful, come for dinner and meet my family."

Later that week, Pastor Schultz visited with Daniel and his family. "There is a state that was established eight years ago in the middle of America called Nebraska," the pastor told Daniel. "It has rich farmland that can be acquired for farming through the Homestead Act of 1862."

"Would we have freedom of religion, and would my sons avoid conscription into the military?" asked Daniel.

"Yes, Protestant churches are being established in Nebraska, and there is no forced military conscription," Pastor Schultz replied. "All you have to do is farm the land."

Everyone in the room quietly stared at the pastor. They all knew that this was where they needed to go. Daniel finally spoke. "It's probably costly to travel there."

"Yes, it is," replied the pastor.

"Thank you, Pastor Schultz. We have a lot to think about," replied Daniel.

After the pastor left, the family discussed their options. Georg was going to turn twenty in a month. He worried daily about having to serve in the military. Daniel worried about his mother's health, and now he would worry about where they would get the money to emigrate. He didn't know if it was possible to leave.

Nevertheless, Daniel decided to receive the appropriate documentation for all family members to travel. He took his family to Saratov before Georg turned twenty so that each of them could receive a Russian passport. The hope was that if they had to leave quickly, they could.

Then one fall Sunday in church, Daniel found out that his friend, Bruno, had decided that his family was going to emigrate to America. "How can you afford this?" asked Daniel.

"I'm selling my cabins, barns, furniture, farm equipment, and animals. I'm selling everything except the land, which I no longer own thanks to the Russians," replied Bruno.

"And you think you will make enough money to go to America?" asked Daniel.

"I must. My son turned twenty in December. We haven't heard anything yet, but we can't stay, because he is not going into the Russian army."

"Georg just turned twenty, and he's a wreck, wondering when they are going to call him up."

"I think it takes a few months, but I'll bet they are gone before they reach the age of twenty-one."

"When is your sale?" asked Daniel.

"Next Saturday," replied Bruno.

"I'll be there. I want to see how you do this."

The next Saturday, Daniel and his boys went to Bruno's sale. Everything was easily sold, even the cabins and barn. There were several young men with families that had no land to farm who were interested in purchasing the homes and then farming the land. Daniel was amazed at how easily everything was sold. "Did you make enough money to fund your trip?" asked Daniel.

"I hope so," replied Bruno. "We have to leave within a week, as my son received his draft card this week and he has to show up for duty in two weeks at the conscription station in Balzer."

"How long did it take to call him up?" asked Daniel.

"He turned twenty in December, and it's now early October. They want him to report November 1," replied Bruno.

"So it takes the Russians about ten months to draft for duty," replied Daniel.

"That's about right," responded Bruno.

"Father, that means they will send me my draft card next April, telling me to report in May," said Georg.

"Don't worry, son, we will figure this out."

After Bruno and his family left, representatives of the German Transatlantic Steam Navigation Line from Hamburg, Germany, visited the villages to offer their services to those who could afford the journey to America. "Are there a lot of families emigrating to America?" asked Daniel.

"Yes, that's why we have come to offer our services, so people can plan their journey," they responded.

"It's an expensive trip," replied Daniel.

"The families who sell everything can afford the trip."

That evening, Daniel told his family about the representatives that he had talked to that day. "This is what we must do, Father," said Georg.

"I know, but your grandmother is too sick to make the trip," replied Daniel.

"We will pray for an answer," said Eva. "God will be our guide."

"At this point, we have another winter to survive," responded Daniel. "Bruno's family left in less than a month when they decided to go, and we can do the same."

Daniel's mother, Elisabeth, was now seventy-seven years old. She had spent most of the last two years in bed and could barely walk. Daniel knew that his mother could not make this trip. After Christmas, Daniel had a talk with Georg. "Son, we cannot go unless your grandmother passes away. She cannot make the trip, and I won't leave her," he said. "However, you can go by yourself, and then we can follow at a later date."

"How will I know where to go?" asked Georg.

"I have a meeting scheduled with Pastor Vogt and some others planning to emigrate. You will go with me," replied Daniel.

As soon as there was a break in snowfall, the men met and discussed the route. As the scouts had done a couple of years earlier, they would take a train to St. Petersburg via Moscow, and then travel to Hamburg by steamship. Then they would travel to America on a Transatlantic Steam Navigation Line steamship to New York. At Castle Garden in New York, they would meet officials of the German Lutheran Immigrant Mission and be directed to travel to this new state of Nebraska.

On the way home after the meeting, Daniel told Georg that he should be prepared to leave by April. "I have enough money for you to make this trip by yourself," said Daniel. "We will make the trip later when we can."

"How will you find me?" asked Georg.

"Talk to Pastor Schultz at the Immigrant Mission. He will help you and then tell us where we can find you when we arrive," replied Daniel.

CHAPTER

18

1876

In March, a few weeks before Georg was scheduled to leave and emigrate to America, Elisabeth passed away. Eva found her.

She ran to find Daniel outside with the boys tending to the animals. "Daniel, it's your mother. Come quickly," she said. Daniel and the boys ran inside the house to Elisabeth's bedroom. Daniel knelt at her bedside. "She looks so peaceful," he said.

"She does," replied Eva.

"She will be the last of us to be buried in Russia," he said.

The family was very busy the next couple of weeks. Not only did they have to plan Elisabeth's funeral but they also needed to plan a sale so that they could emigrate. Georg was no longer leaving by himself. The family would go together.

After Elisabeth's funeral, they held the sale. Again, there were plenty of buyers. Daniel's farms were particularly attractive because they were adjacent lots with three cabins and two barns. In early April 1876, Georg received his draft card with a reporting date of May 1. Two days later, they took a wagon to Saratov and boarded a train to Moscow. Their journey out of Russia had begun.

"This is amazing," exclaimed Friedrich.

"I know. It goes so fast," replied Heinrich.

Daniel and Eva laughed at their boy's fascination with the train. No one in the family had ever been on a train. They weren't used to traveling so fast. None of them had ever traveled beyond Saratov. They were shocked to find out how much countryside existed in Russia.

When they arrived in Moscow, they changed trains to go to St. Petersburg. They were able to sleep on the train, and they had packed food that would last until they reached St. Petersburg. Daniel started thinking about his great-grandparents making this trip across so much land. No one in the family had ever told him about their journey, so he could only imagine the experience.

When they reached St. Petersburg, they were stunned by the size of the city. They knew that they needed to find a place to stay while they arranged passage to Hamburg. Fortunately, Georg had learned enough Russian in the classes that were taught in Merkel a couple of years earlier, as everyone in St. Petersburg spoke only Russian.

Near the shipyard, they found some barracks that served as lodging for those who were waiting for ship passage. Georg was able to speak to the manager and secure room for them in the barracks. Then Georg and Daniel went over to the shipyard to purchase tickets on a ship to Hamburg. They purchased five tickets for departure the next day. "Good thing we didn't have to send you to America by yourself," Daniel said on the way back to the barracks.

"Why do you say that?" asked Georg.

"I don't speak Russian. I couldn't have communicated with these people," replied Daniel. They both laughed, knowing that soon they would be off Russian soil forever.

The next day, they went to the shipyard to board a steamship to Hamburg. Before boarding the ship, their passports were reviewed by a border agent. Everything went well until the agent read Georg's passport. "You are twenty years old," said the agent.

"Yes, I am," replied Georg.

"You are eligible for military conscription. Do you have your draft card?"

"No, I do not. I have not received it yet," replied Georg, lying to the agent.

"Why are you traveling? You will be called up soon," asked the agent.

Georg was so shocked that he couldn't speak. The agent motioned to another agent to take Georg away. Daniel and the rest of the family ran after Georg and the agent. Georg was taken to a room to be questioned by the manager of the border agents. His family wasn't allowed in the room. Daniel was horrified to think that they had come this far only to have his oldest son taken from him. Eva knew that there was only one thing they could do, and that was to pray outside the door. "Our heavenly Father, we beg thee for the return of our son," she began.

When the manager approached the room, he was surprised to see five people praying. "Are those people praying outside your family?" he asked Georg.

"Yes," Georg replied.

"Where are you from?" asked the manager.

"Merkel," replied Georg.

"So you are Germans living along the Volga River?"

"Yes," was Georg's response.

The manager paused and then sighed. "Well, according to the Tsar's decree of 1871, you and your family are allowed to emigrate. If you are not beyond your reporting date for military service, and I believe that you have received a reporting date, then you are allowed to emigrate."

Georg couldn't believe what he was hearing. "I can go?" asked Georg.

"Yes, and go quickly before you miss boarding your ship."

"Thank you," Georg shouted as he ran out of the room. "Hurry, run to the ship," he shouted to his family. They all ran to the ship and were the last to board.

"Will you tell me what is going on?" asked Daniel once they were on the ship.

"The manager told me that since I'm Volga German, the Tsar has decreed that I can emigrate up until the date I'm scheduled to report for military service."

"Our prayers were answered. Thank you, God," replied Eva.

Once they all boarded the ship, it took several minutes for them to recover from what had just happened. Georg knew that he had come very close to being shipped off to serve in the Russian military. They walked around the ship talking about what they had just been through. As the ship left the dock, they realized that they were finally leaving Russia forever. "Finally, we are leaving this country," said Georg.

"And we are never coming back," responded Daniel.

"It is by God's grace that we are all leaving together," added Eva.

"This ship is huge," said Heinrich.

"We could get lost on it," replied Eva, smiling at her son.

"I guess we better figure out where our sleeping quarters are located," said Daniel.

"And where we eat. I'm starving," replied Georg.

"We all are. We've had a rough morning," added Eva.

"Our tickets say that we are third class, so all we need to do is figure out where the third-class passengers sleep," Daniel told them. He stopped a gentleman in a suit and showed him their tickets.

The man looked him up and down. "You are in steerage below deck. You must be immigrants," he sneered.

"Pleasant man," said Georg to Daniel as they walked away. Daniel laughed as they went below deck, where they found a large room filled with beds. Most of them were unclaimed, so it was easy to find six beds together.

"I wonder where we eat," asked Eva.

"And when do we eat?" added Georg.

"Not until this evening," said a voice from across the room. The young man who had spoken walked across the room toward the family. He walked up to Daniel and introduced himself. "My name is Jakob."

"My name is Daniel, and this is my wife, Eva, and my daughter Catherine," replied Daniel. "These are my sons, Georg, Heinrich, and Friedrich."

"Are you traveling alone?" asked Georg.

"Yes," said Jakob. "My family was not able to leave Balzer, but I needed to go because I just turned twenty and I'm now eligible for military service."

Daniel put his hand on Georg's shoulder. "You two young men have something in common."

"We sure do," replied Georg. "I'm twenty as well, and I just received my draft card."

"You did?" asked Jakob. "How long do you have before you report?"

"You report one month after you receive the draft card. I'm supposed to report May 1," replied Georg.

"You came really close to serving," said Jakob.

Georg laughed. "So close that I was nearly not allowed to board this ship."

Jakob was amazed as Georg told the story of his detainment at the port. "Jakob, why don't you bunk over here with us?" said Eva.

"Thank you," he replied.

"Is this your first trip on a ship," asked Daniel.

"Yes, but my uncle was one of the scouts that traveled to America two years ago and he told me everything I need to know about the trip."

"So are you going to Hamburg and then to New York?" asked Georg.

"Yes, I am," replied Jakob.

"Good, we will have plenty of time to talk," responded Georg.

Jakob laughed. "About six weeks of time to talk."

"So how do you know that we don't get to eat until this evening?" asked Daniel.

"I went to the kitchen and asked a cook," responded Jakob.

Georg laughed. "Well, there must be food here somewhere. Let's go, Jakob."

"You two stay out of trouble," said Eva.

"Yes, Mother," replied Georg as they ran off.

Daniel, Eva, Catherine, Heinrich, and Friedrich decided to take a walk on the main deck as well. They found that they weren't allowed to be in certain areas. Apparently, since they were in the steerage class, they couldn't be near the first-class cabins. At least they were able to get above deck and get some fresh air.

That evening, they found out what they would be eating twice a day for the next two weeks. They would have boiled meats and vegetables brought to them and would serve themselves. Fortunately, they had been told to bring their own eating utensils because there were no bowls or forks available for their use. The scouts had warned future immigrants of this, and Eva had made sure her family was prepared. Jakob was also prepared.

There was no table to sit at, so everyone sat on their bed to eat. None of this seemed to matter to them, as they thanked God for the nourishment and prayed for a safe journey.

That night, they all struggled to sleep. Even with blankets, they were cold. Steerage was below the waterline, so it was cold and damp. All night long, they were kept awake by the sound of the sea hitting the ship. "Maybe we should move the beds together so our body heat will keep us warmer," said Daniel the next morning.

"It's worth a try," responded Eva.

They tried this the next night, and it helped, somewhat. Eventually, everyone adjusted to the conditions. They had been blessed with calm seas and winds for most of their trip. Daniel wondered what the trip was like for his great-grandparents. He knew that they were originally from Hamburg, but he knew nothing about their trip to Merkel.

Once they reached the North Sea, it started to rain. It rained for several days, and the sea became rougher, which made conditions more challenging in steerage. No one wanted to get wet on the main deck, so they stayed below for several days. On several occasions, the hatches were sealed to prevent water from getting in. It was stuffy, and the air was foul-smelling.

When the rain stopped, everyone was eager to leave steerage and walk on the main deck. "It's so wonderful to see the sun again," exclaimed Eva.

"The only difference between what we just endured and the Russian winter is that this didn't last forever," replied Daniel.

Georg and Jakob were walking toward them. "We just found out that we will arrive in Hamburg tomorrow," said Georg.

"Wonderful," replied Daniel. That evening, everyone was in a joyful mood knowing that their time on this ship was about to end.

The next afternoon, they sailed into the port of Hamburg. Upon disembarking from the ship, they went to purchase tickets on the ship to New York. They found out that all the ships were full that were leaving in the next couple of days, so they were going to have to stay in Hamburg for two nights. Again, their tickets were third class.

They were told by the ticket agent to be at the dock early because the ship was completely booked.

They then went to the barracks, adjacent to the shipyards, to arrange beds for the next two nights. They had plenty of time to walk around Hamburg and purchase food. "This is where my great-grandparents are from," said Daniel to the boys.

"Father, do you know why they left?" asked Heinrich.

"I was told that great-grandfather Christoph had fought in a war, and he wasn't going to do it again," replied Daniel.

"My family left Germany because of religious persecution," stated Eva. "The Catholics and the Protestants could not get along together."

"Mother, were they from Hamburg?" asked Friedrich.

"No, they were from Bremen. I really don't know much about them."

"It seems like no one talked about anything other than life in Russia," added Daniel.

"It's strange that we are walking through the city that they left," said Georg.

Daniel laughed. "It probably looks nothing like it did then. Well, let's go back to the barracks for the evening. We can do more exploring tomorrow."

CHAPTER
19

The next morning, they set out to see other sites in the city. "Look at the large clock tower over there!" exclaimed Georg, pointing in the direction of a tall tower.

"Let's go see it," replied Daniel.

They walked a couple of blocks to the front of a church. They stood in front of the church, gazing at it in astonishment. "I wonder if we can go inside," asked Jakob.

They walked up the steps and pushed on the door. It opened and they went inside. They were speechless. They had never seen anything like this. As they walked farther inside, they saw a huge pulpit with a magnificent staircase leading to it in the center of the room. There were pipes hanging on one of the walls, but they had no idea why they were there. The stone was gorgeous. It looked polished. They sat in one of the pews, breathlessly stunned by the beauty.

A man walked from the side of the church to greet them. "Hello, I'm Pastor Müller. Welcome to St. Michael's Lutheran Church."

Finally, Daniel replied. "This is a Lutheran church?"

"Yes, it is," replied the pastor.

"How old is it?"

"It dates back to the mid-1600s. It was built not long after the Reformation," stated Pastor Müller. "Where are you from?"

"We are from Russia. We were living along the Volga River, and now we are immigrating to America," replied Daniel. "My great-grandparents were from Hamburg, and they emigrated to Russia."

"Interesting," replied the pastor. "We keep records of everyone baptized and married in the church. I can look for your family if you wish."

"Sure, their names were Christoph and Maria Bauer," said Daniel.

"I will go look." When Pastor Müller returned, he had a smile on his face. "Well, Daniel, your great-grandfather Christoph was baptized in 1724, and he and Maria were married in 1744."

"In this church?" asked Daniel.

"In a much smaller version of this church," replied the pastor.

"Oh my," exclaimed Eva in amazement. Daniel just stared at the pastor, not knowing what to say.

"I know this is very shocking. It looks like your great-grandparents were Lutheran," Pastor Müller continued.

"We are Lutheran, and our village, Merkel in Russia, is comprised of only Lutherans. Apparently, the Russians wanted to avoid religious conflicts, so the villages were established based upon religion," replied Daniel.

"When are you sailing to America?" asked the pastor.

"Tomorrow," said Daniel.

"Let us pray for your safe journey to America," responded Pastor Müller.

When they left the church, they stood outside the gates, amazed at what they had just experienced. "Father, what are the chances that we would find information about your great-grandparents?" asked Georg.

"I know. This has been truly remarkable," replied Daniel. "We have a big day tomorrow, so let's get back to the barracks and eat so we can be rested for tomorrow."

The next morning, they went to the shipyard and stood in line to board the ship. "It's a good thing we came early," said Georg.

"Yes, it is. Look how long this line is," added Jakob. "There are going to be a lot of people on this ship."

When they boarded the ship, they went below deck to steerage as quickly as they could. They wanted to find seven beds together. People were already taking most of the beds. They managed to find five beds together with two beds a short distance away. Georg and Jakob took those two beds, with the rest of the family taking the other five. "This could be a rough trip," said Eva.

"God will be with us. We will survive," responded Daniel. There was too much chaos for them to walk along the main deck, so they sat on their beds and talked until the ship set sail.

Steerage was packed with people, many more than the ship from St. Petersburg. The line for dinner was so long that by the time they received their food, it was cold. Sleeping was also difficult with so many people. At least they weren't as cold as on the previous trip.

For the first few days, the weather was pleasant, and they were able to spend most of their day on the main deck. During this time, they sailed past several large white rocks. They were told that these were icebergs that had cleaved off large islands of ice farther north. "They're amazing," stated Heinrich.

"I could stay up here on deck and watch them all day," responded Friedrich.

"I was told that by tomorrow, we won't be seeing them anymore, so enjoy them, boys," laughed Georg.

By the second week on the ship, storms could be seen on the horizon. The next day, it started to rain, and all steerage passengers had to be locked below deck. The hatches were sealed, and it was clear very early that there were too many people in the room. The stuffy, foul-smelling air became unbearable. People became seasick and started spending all their time in bed. Catherine became so ill that she couldn't eat anything. Eva found herself caring for her daughter night and day.

Finally, almost a week later, the storm broke, and the skies cleared. The hatches were unlocked, and everyone who could still walk went up to the main deck. Daniel and Georg helped Catherine up to the main deck so that she could see the sun and get some fresh air. The sea breezes were now warmer than they had been in Hamburg. "I wonder if we are getting close to America," said Daniel.

"I hope so, Father, as I can't take much more of this," replied Catherine.

"Try to eat some food tonight," said Eva. "You need to have your strength for when we get to America."

"My uncle said that all immigrants must be healthy, or they won't let you stay in the country," added Jakob.

"Then we will have to nurse Catherine back to health," replied Eva.

With each passing day, Catherine became stronger. Meanwhile, they all prayed that there would be no more storms. They were running low on food in steerage, so the entire family shared their food with Catherine so she would have her strength when they reached New York.

Finally, almost four weeks after they left Hamburg, they docked in New York. Immediately after they disembarked, they were taken to immigration, where they were asked questions. Fortunately, some of the immigration agents spoke German, as no one in the family spoke English. "What is your name?" the agent asked Daniel.

"Daniel Bauer," replied Daniel.

"Where were you born?"

"Merkel, Russia."

"Have you ever been in jail?"

"No."

"What was your job in Russia?"

"Farmer."

"Do you know anyone in this country?"

"No."

"How do you know where you are going?"

"We are going to the Immigrant Mission at Castle Garden for guidance," replied Daniel.

"Once you are examined by the doctor, you can proceed to the mission," the agent stated.

Everyone in the family went through this questioning. Then they were sent to the line waiting for the physician to examine them.

Once they reached the front of the line, the doctor examined their scalp, face, neck, and hands. Heinrich and Friedrich were pulled out of the line and taken to the side before the doctor could examine them. "What are you doing? Where are you taking them?" demanded Daniel.

"Adolescents and children are examined separately," the agent stated in English. Someone near Daniel tried to translate for him.

Daniel and Eva were fearful that the boys would be taken from them, as Georg was in St. Petersburg.

They were finished with the medical exam and were being pushed along when they spotted the two boys. Daniel could see the panic in his son's eyes as he ran toward them. They embraced and hugged, while the rest of the family navigated through the crowd to get to them. "That was close," said Daniel. "We are not going to let anything like that happen again."

"We are now officially in America, so hopefully there will be no more attempts to separate us," said Georg.

"Let's make our way to the Immigrant Mission," replied Daniel. "Perhaps we will see Pastor Schultz."

Once they reached the mission, they looked for Pastor Schultz. He was across the room speaking with a family. "I guess this is where we part ways," said Jakob. "I will be purchasing train tickets to travel to family that I have in Iowa."

They all said their goodbyes to Jakob and wished him a safe trip. "May God be with you," replied Georg as Jakob departed.

By the time they finished, Pastor Schultz was available, so they walked across the room to greet him. "Hello, Pastor Schultz," Daniel said, shaking his hand. "You probably don't remember me."

"Yes, Daniel, I do remember you. Welcome to America."

"We are hoping to get information on settling in Nebraska," said Daniel.

"We have put together an itinerary for immigrants," replied the pastor. "We will take your family to the train station in a horse-drawn carriage, and then you will take the train to Chicago. In Chicago, you will change trains and board a train to Omaha, Nebraska. Once you reach Omaha, you will board a Burlington and Missouri River Railroad train to Lincoln. When you arrive in Lincoln, you will visit the Burlington Land Office, where you will be able to claim land to farm."

"It sounds simple enough," replied Daniel.

"It is simple. Welcome to America," laughed Pastor Schultz. "Gather your things and stand in that line over there to await a carriage to the train station."

CHAPTER

20

Daniel and his family stood in line waiting for a carriage for almost an hour. They spent the time chatting, but most of the time was spent watching other people. The mission was a very busy place.

When they boarded their carriage, Eva remarked, "It seems like it has been years since we used this form of transportation."

The others laughed. "And soon, we will be back to traveling by train," added Georg.

When they reached the train station, Daniel went to the ticket office to purchase six tickets to Chicago. They had very little time before the train left, so they found the train and boarded as quickly as possible. The train car was nearly full, so they were unable to sit together. Daniel, Eva, and Catherine sat together, and the three boys sat closer to the front. The boys were unable to sit together, so they took any available seat they could find.

Once the train started to move, the conductor gathered the tickets from the passengers. Heinrich felt very uncomfortable because the young man next to him kept making faces at him. Then the man jumped up and yelled, "You stink. You're a filthy immigrant." Heinrich had no idea what the man said, but he knew that he was mad. Georg got up out of his seat and ran to Heinrich's aid. By this time, the man was pushing and shoving Heinrich out of his seat.

"What is your problem?" asked Georg in German as he tried to grab the man.

"Ah, we have a Fritz here. Let go of me, you filthy German pig," the man yelled.

Soon others joined in the fight. Daniel ran to the front of the train to grab his boys. Finally, the conductor showed up and started yelling at everyone. Daniel and his family understood nothing of what was being said. The conductor could see that he was getting nowhere, so he pointed to three English-speaking people sitting near Daniel, Eva, and Catherine and told them to move to the seats occupied by Heinrich, Friedrich, and Georg. He motioned to the three boys to take the vacant seats closer to the rest of the family. He then said to everyone in the car, "If there is any more fighting on this train, I will throw the perpetrators off this train in the middle of nowhere, and believe me, there is a lot of nowhere between New York and Chicago."

A few minutes later after the conductor left, Daniel went to speak with his boys. "You will stay away from those men upfront for the rest of this trip. I will arrive in Chicago with my sons."

"How long will it take to get to Chicago?" asked Friedrich.

"I don't know," replied Daniel.

The gentleman sitting next to Friedrich spoke German. "One week," he stated. They all shook their heads. They were exhausted, and it was starting to show.

"I will help you watch over your sons," said the gentleman.

"Thank you," replied Daniel. "My name is Daniel."

"Ludwig."

"Thank you for your help, Ludwig," said Daniel as he returned to his seat.

Once Daniel sat down, he told Eva and Catherine that they would be on this train for a week. They both sighed. "I suppose we are expected to spend the whole week on these hard benches," said Eva.

"I hope not, Mother," replied Catherine.

A couple of hours later, the train pulled into a train station. The conductor announced that they would be there for an hour before the train left. He told them that they were in Philadelphia and that the train would not stop again until they reached Pittsburgh. Ludwig translated for Daniel and his family, adding, "Now is a good time to get food."

Daniel and his family left the train, following the other immigrants to stand in line to receive food. "Our food is much cheaper than the food they get in first class," said Ludwig.

"I wonder what it's like to travel in first class," said Daniel.

"It's very nice and eloquent. They have tables to eat at and beds to sleep in," replied Ludwig.

"I wouldn't know how to behave in such a place."

Ludwig laughed. "Don't worry, they wouldn't let the likes of us immigrants on their train car anyway."

They both laughed. "Where are you from?" asked Daniel.

"Berlin," replied Ludwig.

"We are from Russia. We farmed along the Volga River."

"I'm a Lutheran pastor," replied Ludwig.

"Oh, where are you going?"

"Nebraska," responded Ludwig. "Lutheran churches are being established, but there is a shortage of pastors who speak German."

"That's wonderful. We are Lutheran, and we are going to Nebraska," replied Daniel. "Maybe you will be the pastor of the church that we attend."

Ludwig smiled. "Maybe."

"Now that we have our food, we better head back to the train," added Eva.

The train left the station and traveled toward Pittsburgh. In the evening, it became dark in the train cabin, and everyone tried to sleep. The benches were hardwood, and there wasn't enough room for everyone to lie down; so most tried to sleep sitting up. After several days of this, everyone was so exhausted that it was easier for most to sleep sitting up.

Finally, five days after they left New York, they arrived in Chicago. When they left the train, they went to the ticket office to purchase tickets to Omaha. They were told the next train to Omaha wouldn't leave until tomorrow and that there was an immigrant hotel across the street from the station.

The hotel had a large room with multiple beds. "It looks like our accommodations on the ships," said Georg.

"It will definitely be more comfortable than sitting up and sleeping," replied Heinrich. They all agreed.

"Well, tomorrow we get back on a train, so we better get plenty of rest tonight," stated Daniel.

The next morning, they left the hotel and went to a market to purchase food to eat on the train to Omaha. When they boarded the train, they noticed there was plenty of room, and they were all able to sit together. There were more families, and many of them spoke German. Most were headed west to homestead land.

As they traveled west, they noticed more and more open land. "I wonder how much land will be available to us in Nebraska," stated Georg.

"Given the vast land here, I'm sure there will be plenty for the taking in Nebraska," replied Daniel.

Two days later, they arrived in Omaha. They gathered their belongings and went to the Burlington and Missouri River Railroad ticket office and purchased tickets to Lincoln. They were told that their train would leave that evening and travel overnight to Lincoln, arriving the next morning. "This is it. This is the last night on a train," Daniel told his family when he returned with the tickets. They all smiled, knowing that by this time tomorrow they would be at their destination.

As they waited to board their train, Daniel asked Ludwig about his plans. "I will go to the Burlington Land Office, and they will take me to the village I will be serving," replied Ludwig.

"We are to go to the same office to be given free land," stated Daniel. "I hope that you are the pastor of our church."

They boarded the train and noticed immediately that there was more room for sleeping. "This is a much newer train than the ones we have been on previously," stated Eva.

"The benches have cushions," added Catherine.

"Finally, our last night on a train, we have comfort," Daniel laughed.

The next morning, they arrived at the train station in Lincoln. When they left the train, they immediately went to the Burlington Land Office. There was already a line forming outside the office. It took almost two hours for them to reach the front of the line. As they drew closer, they became more and more anxious.

Finally, it was Daniel's turn to go inside. Ludwig went with him to translate. "I am here with my family to homestead land," Daniel said.

"Where are you from?" asked the clerk.

"Merkel, Russia, along the Volga River," replied Daniel.

"What did you do there?"

"Farming."

"Wonderful! We have land for you," replied the clerk. "We have free land for homesteading within the limits of our land grant. We can give you 160 acres, and all you need to do is build a house and farm the land for five years. You also need to go through the process of becoming an American citizen."

Daniel nodded his head, smiling.

"Do you have family?" asked the clerk.

"Yes, I have a wife and four children, three sons and a daughter."

"Good. Give me a few minutes to process your land deed," stated the clerk.

A few minutes later, Daniel received the deed to his new land. He went outside and showed it to his family. "Today we reap the rewards of God's blessings," he told his family.

"Praise be to God, for he has kept us safe throughout this journey," added Eva.

Soon after, Ludwig came out the door and announced that he would be the pastor in the Lutheran church in the new village that was being established. "Then you will be our pastor," asked Daniel.

"Yes, I will," replied Ludwig.

"This is truly a blessed day," exclaimed Eva.

"Yes, it is. Let us pray, thanking God," said Ludwig as he led the group in prayer.

About the Author

Merribeth Bruntz is a Christian who lives with her family in Colorado. She is an avid bicyclist, master gardener, and retired podiatrist.